"It's hard for you to see the prison, isn't it?"

Hunter opened his mouth to deny it, but somehow the lie caught in his throat.

"I lost two and a half years there. It's a little hard to get past that."

Kate's blue eyes softened with understanding, and she reached a hand across the SUV and touched his arm with gentle fingers. "I'm so sorry, Hunter."

He jerked his arm away. "I'm sorry enough for myself. I don't need your pity, too."

She paled as if he had slapped her and quickly pulled her hand away. "Right. Of course you don't."

He opened his mouth to apologize, then closed it again. Maybe it was better this way. It was going to be tough enough for him to stay away from her on their journey without having to endure shared confidences and these casual touches that would destroy him....

Dear Reader,

Get ready for this month's romantic adrenaline rush from Silhouette Intimate Moments. First up, we have RITA® Award-winning author Kathleen Creighton's next STARRS OF THE WEST book, *Secret Agent Sam* (#1363), a high-speed, action-packed romance with a tough-as-nails heroine you'll never forget. RaeAnne Thayne delivers the next book in her emotional miniseries THE SEARCHERS, *Never Too Late* (#1364), which details a heroine's search for the truth about her mysterious past…and an unexpected detour in love.

As part of Karen Whiddon's intriguing series THE PACK— about humans who shape-shift into wolves—*One Eye Closed* (#1365) tells the story of a wife who is in danger and turns to the only man who can help: her enigmatic husband. Kylie Brant heats up our imagination in *The Business of Strangers* (#1366), where a beautiful amnesiac falls for the last man on earth she should love— a reputed enemy!

Linda Randall Wisdom enthralls us with *After the Midnight Hour* (#1367), a story of a heart-stopping detective's fierce attraction to a tormented woman…who was murdered by her husband a century ago! Can this impossible love overcome the bonds of time? And don't miss Loreth Anne White's *The Sheik Who Loved Me* (#1368), in which a dazzling spy falls for the sexy sheik she's supposed to be investigating. So, what will win out—duty or true love?

Live and love the excitement in Silhouette Intimate Moments, where emotion meets high-stakes romance. And be sure to join us next month for another stellar lineup.

Happy reading!

Patience Smith
Associate Senior Editor

Please address questions and book requests to:
Silhouette Reader Service
U.S.: 3010 Walden Ave., P.O. Box 1325, Buffalo, NY 14269
Canadian: P.O. Box 609, Fort Erie, Ont. L2A 5X3

Never Too Late

RaeANNE THAYNE

INTIMATE MOMENTS™

Published by Silhouette Books

America's Publisher of Contemporary Romance

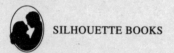 **SILHOUETTE BOOKS**

ISBN 0-373-27434-3

NEVER TOO LATE

Printed in U.S.A.

Books by RaeAnne Thayne

RAEANNE THAYNE

lives in a graceful old Victorian nestled in the rugged mountains of northern Utah, along with her husband and two young children. Her books have won numerous honors, including several readers' choice awards and a RITA® Award nomination by the Romance Writers of America. RaeAnne loves to hear from readers. She can be reached through her Web site at www.raeannethayne.com or at P.O. Box 6682, North Logan, UT 84341.

For Kjersten Thayne, the best daughter in the world!
I couldn't have written this one without you.

Chapter 1

What was wrong with her? Kate Spencer wondered as she watched her brother twirl her best friend—his new wife—around the room. The small train of Taylor's elegantly simple ivory gown brushed the floor and her face glowed with joy at being in the arms of the man she loved.

They looked perfect together, the lanky cowboy author and his lovely, serene bride. But instead of sighing over the romance of the moment, Kate only felt restless, edgy, uncomfortable inside her skin.

She sipped at her champagne as an odd combination of emotions floated through her veins along with the bubbles.

She was thrilled for Wyatt and Taylor. How could anyone look at the two of them together and not be thrilled for them? She loved Taylor and wanted her friend to be happy and though she couldn't say she'd really had the chance to get to know her brother in the nearly six weeks since he had found her, her gut told her Wyatt was a good man who would rather cut off his arm than hurt his new bride.

And there was the cause of her restlessness—that she didn't really know Wyatt at all. She shifted and set the flute on the table. Wyatt was her flesh and blood yet she barely knew him. Or her other brother Gage or their parents, Lynn and Sam.

She was suddenly overflowing with family. A mother, a father, two strong, handsome brothers. And now two sisters-in-law and even two step-nieces from Gage's marriage to Allie DeBarillas.

For a woman who had grown up believing she was nothing—less than nothing, just the throwaway kid of a homeless junkie—this sudden surplus of relations was daunting.

Intellectually she knew she belonged here with them. DNA tests proved without a doubt that she was the child of Sam and Lynn McKinnon, sister to Gage and Wyatt. But emotionally, they were still all strangers to her, all but Taylor.

If circumstances had been different, she would have known that her father wasn't very graceful on the dance floor and that Gage and Wyatt both looked strong and masculine and gorgeous in their tuxedos.

She would have known her mother didn't drink anything stronger than white wine and that Gage had broken both his legs earlier in the summer and that Sam had the incredible skills to carve the delicate wood angel that graced the soaring twenty-foot-high Christmas tree.

She was only now just learning all of those things because her entire life with these people had been stolen from her one hot summer afternoon twenty-three years ago.

She needed to move, to channel some of this restless energy into something constructive.

As Taylor's maid of honor, shouldn't she be doing something? Mingling or labeling gifts or helping out in the kitchen? She jumped up, intent on finding something to occupy her mind beyond her own problems. Before she could escape, though, Lynn whirled past her in the arms of her oldest son Gage.

Blond and petite, Lynn looked radiant and far too young to have two sons in their thirties, one a decorated FBI agent and one a bestselling true-crime author.

And a daughter, Kate had to remind herself, a daughter who barely knew her.

Bitterness welled up inside her and threatened to spill out but she staunchly suppressed it just as Lynn disengaged from her son's arms and wrapped Kate in a sweet-scented embrace. Her mother was a toucher, she was discovering. Lynn rarely let a conversation go by without holding her arm or squeezing her hand or patting her knee.

Kate had wondered more than once if perhaps Lynn needed somehow to make up for the twenty-three years they'd been apart, for all the hugs and kisses they had missed. Or maybe she was afraid if she didn't touch her to make sure she was real, Kate would once more disappear.

"Hasn't this been the most wonderful day?" Lynn beamed. "I'm so happy I just want to dance all night."

Kate managed a smile and hugged her back. "It's lovely. Everything is perfect. I don't know how you and Taylor threw this together on such short notice."

Lynn laughed. "We didn't have any choice. Wyatt refused to wait once he found his Taylor. Gage was the same way."

Gage smiled at both of them and Kate thought again how ruggedly handsome the FBI agent was. "We McKinnon men are impatient creatures," he said. "Once we find what we want, we move fast."

She watched his gaze scan the room until it rested on his wife, Allie, who was laughing as she tried to show her daughter Gabriella the steps of a waltz. Allie didn't seem to mind Gaby's shiny black Mary Janes planted on top of her own evening shoes as she moved through the dance.

Gage smiled at them both and the love in his eyes blazed brighter than all the stacks of candles gleaming around the room.

Kate knew Gage and Allie had been married for three months but they still acted as if they couldn't bear to be out of each other's sight. She hadn't been there, of course. She hadn't even known she had a pair of brothers three months earlier.

"I'm sorry I missed your wedding," she said on impulse, then regretted it when Lynn hugged her again, her eyes sorrowful.

"Oh my darling. We're just so glad you're here now. It seems like a dream, the most wonderful of miracles, that we've found you again after all these years. And just in time for the holidays!"

Kate blew out a breath. She had barely given Christmas a thought between helping Taylor with her wedding, finishing up her E.R. rotation in her second year of residency and dealing with this wild tangle of emotions at learning her true identity.

Finding out she had been kidnapped at the age of three from the arms of a loving family and thrust into the hell she'd lived as a child tended to make everything else on her to-do list fade into the background. How was she supposed to adjust to the fact that the person she thought she was all her life didn't exist?

She supposed she needed somehow to summon the energy and get busy about the holidays. It was unlike her to procrastinate so long—her friends always teased that she usually had her shopping done by Halloween.

Though she typically only bought a few gifts—something for Taylor and a few other friends, and for Tom and Maryanne Spencer, her foster parents in St. Petersburg—she was stunned by the sudden realization that her list had now grown by leaps and bounds.

She already had something for Taylor, a stained-glass wall hanging she had purchased at the arts festival in Park City last August, but now she would have to find something for Lynn and Sam, for Wyatt, for Gage, and for Allie and her children.

Before she could give in to the panic spurting through her at the idea, Lynn squeezed her hands. "I know I've mentioned this at least a dozen times before," her mother went on, "but I wanted to remind you again that I'm having dinner Christmas Eve at my home in Liberty. We'll all be together. Even Sam is staying until after the holidays."

A blush stole across Lynn's still-lovely skin like autumn's touch on a delicate leaf and Kate wondered at it. She looked for her father and found him on the dance floor with Allie's youngest daughter, Anna.

Sam McKinnon was still a handsome man, she thought, even though he was probably nearing sixty. He was exactly the kind of man she would have selected for a father if she'd been given a chance—quiet and strong, with powerful shoulders, a deep desert tan from years of living in Las Vegas, and the nicked and callused hands of a carpenter.

Her parents had divorced decades ago, a year after she'd been kidnapped. Could Lynn still have feelings for Sam after all this time? And if she did, why had she never acted on them?

Did their divorce stem from the trauma of losing a child?

Though she knew it was irrational, she couldn't help a pang of guilt, as if somehow she had been responsible.

"We'll be eating around seven," Lynn said. "A little early because of the girls."

"I'm looking forward to it," she lied smoothly.

The fact that her words were a lie only made her more angry. These were wonderful people—loving and kind and painfully eager for her to take her place in their family. Why couldn't she? Why was she so damn conflicted every time she saw the love in their eyes?

Why couldn't she become the daughter they had lost?

Sam suddenly swung Anna around in their direction through the crowd to join them. The moment they were close enough, Anna jumped from his arms and threw her arms around Gage's waist.

"Gage-Gage-Gage," she chattered. "Grandpa Sam and me were dancing. He says I dance just like Clara in *The Nutcracker.* Wanta see?"

She didn't give him a chance to answer as she pulled him out to the area of the room that had been cleared of furniture for dancing.

"Looks like I've lost my partner," Sam said with that warm smile of his. "How about if I take my beautiful little girl for a spin around the dance floor instead?"

She gazed at that smile. How many other dances had she missed with her father over the years? What would her life have been like if she'd had Sam, with his broad hands and his warm smile, to help her over all the rough patches along the way?

She thought of the times when her home had been the back seat of a broken-down car, when her stomach had churned with hunger more often than not, when her only friend had been a tattered doll Brenda had picked up at the Salvation Army during one of her good moods.

Suddenly she couldn't bear this. She cared about these people and she wanted to love them. But how could she, when she couldn't see past her own bitterness over all that had been taken from her?

She blew out a breath, loathe to disappoint this kind man more than she feared she already had been a great disappointment to all of them. "Um, I'm a bit warm. I think I need to sneak out for a little air. Do you mind?"

"Not at all, honey." He winked at her and slipped an arm across Lynn's shoulders. "I've been waiting all night for my chance to sweep the mother of the groom off her feet."

Lynn blushed again but went willingly into his arms. Neither of them noticed as Kate slipped through the huge gathering room of the Bradshaws' ski lodge in Little Cottonwood Canyon with its heavy log beams and soaring cathedral ceiling.

The large home was the perfect place for a December wedding. Besides the huge tree in front of the floor-to-ceiling windows, with its twinkling gold lights and plump burgundy ribbons, more lights winked from fresh garlands hanging on the stairway and around the doorways. Gold and burgundy candles speared out of more greenery on the mantel of the huge rock fireplace, where a fire burned merrily.

It was a magical scene, one she would have delighted in for Taylor if circumstances had been different. She barely noticed, though, as she hurried through the house and slipped out the door leading to the wide deck that circled the rear of the house.

The twinkling lights extended out here and gave her just enough light to pick her way carefully across the deck. The December cold was a welcome relief from the warm house and from the heat of her own emotions as she leaned against the railing and lifted her face to the gentle snowfall.

After a moment, she could feel the tension in her shoulders begin to seep away as tiny flakes caught on the mossy-green velvet of her dress, in her hair, on her eyelashes. She relaxed enough that she even stuck her tongue out to catch a few stray snowflakes.

Growing up in Florida, she'd never seen snow as a child. It wasn't until she came to Utah for college that she had experienced her first snowfall and she still remembered how entranced she'd been by the sheer beauty of it.

Eight years later, she'd seen enough snow for it to lose much of its magic—it was mostly just a pain to drive in and a hassle to scrape off her car on her way to class or to the hospital.

Until moments like this.

Inside, the string quartet played something low and lovely and the mountains gleamed white in the moonlight. Tiny, gentle snowflakes kissed her cheeks.

She wasn't sure how long she stood there, but she did know this was the nearest thing to peace she had known since Wyatt had revealed to her the results of the DNA testing he had secretly ordered after they'd met through Taylor.

"You stay out here much longer, you're going to catch pneumonia."

The voice from the darkness startled her and she whirled so quickly she nearly lost her footing on the snow-slick wood of the deck. A large, dark shape stepped out of the shadows at the edge of the deck and into the light spilling from the lodge windows.

She recognized Hunter Bradshaw, Taylor's older brother, and pressed a hand to her suddenly racing heart. To her chagrin, she suddenly wasn't sure if her increased pulse stemmed from being caught unawares or from suddenly finding herself in such close proximity to Hunter.

In a dark suit and white shirt, he was gorgeous, with dark hair the color of hot cocoa, lean, elegant features and dark-blue eyes that gleamed in the night. And, she had to admit, he had been making her pulse race since they'd met five years earlier.

"Sorry," he said. "Didn't mean to scare you."

"I didn't realize anyone else was here." Her voice sounded breathless and she cleared her throat to conceal her reaction to him. "How long have you been standing there?".

"Oh, about fifteen minutes before you showed up."

He had watched her the whole time? While she lifted her face to the sky and caught snowflakes on her tongue like a kid on the playground at recess? Heat rushed to her cheeks, surely enough to melt any flakes left there.

"I'm sorry I interrupted your solitude."

"Don't worry about it," he finally said after an odd pause.

"I'll leave. You obviously wanted to be alone."

He shrugged. "Not really. I just can't seem to spend enough time outside."

He didn't add any other explanation, but he didn't need to. She knew exactly why he craved fresh air, even cold and snowy fresh air. It all must seem heavenly to a man who had only been out of prison for a little over a month.

Hunter had spent more than two years on death row for a hideous crime he didn't commit. He had only gained his freedom after Taylor and Wyatt had uncovered the truth behind the slayings of Hunter's pregnant girlfriend, her mother and her unborn child.

Relieved to be able to focus on someone else's problems for a change, she studied him in the moon's glow and the twinkling lights. He looked tired, she thought, and the doctor in her wondered how he'd been sleeping since his release.

"How are you doing? I mean, really doing?"

He was quiet for a moment, as if not very many people had asked him that. "When I was first released," he finally said, "I wanted to do everything I'd been dreaming about inside that miserable cell for thirty-one months. I wanted to climb the Tetons again and feel the water rushing around my waders as I stood in a stream with a fly rod and ski every single black diamond run I could find."

"Did you?"

His laugh was rueful and a little bitter. "The first week. Now for some strange reason I can't seem to generate enough energy to do anything but sit out here and breathe the mountain air."

She knew exactly what he meant—his discontent and malaise mirrored her own.

"You've been through a terrible ordeal. It's going to take a while to adjust to normalcy again. Give yourself a little time."

Hunter had to smile at that crisp, professional note in her voice. "Thank you, Dr. Spencer. I don't believe I realized psychiatric medicine was your specialty."

He watched as color climbed her high cheekbones and wondered if Taylor had any clue how very much she resembled Lynn McKinnon.

"You know it's not," she said. "But in family medicine you need to do a little of everything. Sorry for the uninvited advice. Hazard of the profession. I'm afraid I always think I know what's best for everyone."

"No, I appreciate it. Intellectually I know you're right— I just need more time to adjust. But I've never been a particularly patient man and I'm having a hard time trying to figure myself out right now."

He paused, uncomfortable talking about this with anyone,

but especially with Kate Spencer, and decided to change the subject. "Taylor tells me you're doing well with your residency."

"Right. I just finished an E.R. rotation and on Christmas Day I start one in the neonatal intensive care unit at Primary Children's Medical Center."

He hadn't been a cop for a while now but even his rusty detective skills could hear the definite lack of enthusiasm in her voice and he wondered at it. As long as he had known her, Kate had been focused on only one thing—becoming a doctor. It had been the strongest tie binding her to his sister, the common ground that had led them to becoming friends.

"You don't sound very thrilled about it."

"I am. I've been looking forward to working in the NICU. I know I'll gain valuable skills there."

"But?"

She sighed and turned back to the ghostly mountains. "But just like you, I can't seem to work up much enthusiasm for anything right now."

"You've had a wild few months, I guess."

"We both have."

They drifted into a comfortable silence. After a moment, she stirred next to him and he caught the scent of her, that mouthwatering smell of vanilla sugar, and suddenly became *very* uncomfortable.

With her blond hair piled up on her head and that slender green dress, she looked elegant and graceful and delicious. He wondered what Dr. Spencer would do if he gave in to his sudden urge to yank the pins out of those luscious curls, bury his fingers in them, and pull her toward him.

He hadn't had much to do with women since his release and his body was loudly reminding him of the fact.

That had certainly been on his to-do list, one of those things he'd dreamed about in prison—sex with a different woman every single day for a month.

But the reality was, he didn't enjoy meaningless sex. He'd had plenty of offers since his release from prison but all from the kind of women who didn't appeal to him at all, the kind who found his dark history a turn-on and wanted to make it with an ex-con, even an innocent one.

He cleared his throat and tried to figure out how he could escape without being rude.

"Do you think you'll take your old job back?" she asked, unaware of his torment.

If any question could deflate his fledgling lust, it was that one. He stared out into the night. "That's still one of those things in the undecided column. I don't know."

"You were a good cop, Hunter."

"Yeah, I was." He didn't say it out of ego. "I loved it. But I have to admit I don't have much faith left in the system."

How could he, when that system he'd worked so hard to uphold had failed him so miserably? Despite an unblemished—even stellar—career with the Salt Lake City Police Department, he had first been arrested and then convicted of taking three lives, one of them an unborn child, one a dying cancer patient and one the woman he thought he loved.

He would still be in that cell on death row if not for his sister's unwavering faith in him. God knows, his former buddies on the force had all turned on him. The system of justice he had built his life around had failed him with disastrous consequences, and he didn't know if he could ever believe in it again.

And if he didn't believe in it, he sure as hell couldn't pick up his detective shield again and take up where he had left off before his arrest nearly three years earlier.

"So what will you do?" Kate asked.

He shrugged. "For now, I guess I'll just stay out here and watch the mountains."

She laughed a little, then shivered as a cold gust of wind blew across the porch. "We're both going to turn into blocks of ice if we stay out here much longer."

"I suppose we'd better go inside."

He was surprised to see her expression become guarded, reluctant.

"Why the hesitation? That's your family in there."

"I don't know. I must be crazy, right?"

He gave a harsh laugh. "Believe me, I know crazy. You can't spend thirty-one months behind bars and not get real good at telling the nuts from the wackos. You're neither— in fact, you're one of the most sane women I know."

"Not the last six weeks. I'm a mess, Hunter."

She faced him then and he was stunned to see tears gathering in her vivid blue eyes. He didn't know what to do for a wild moment, then he placed a hand over hers, struck by her icy fingers.

He squeezed her hand and she gave him a tremulous smile. They stood there for a moment, then she slipped her hand away and returned to the deck railing.

"I should be happy. I *know* I should. I'm suddenly surrounded by this wonderful family, people who love me and want me to be part of their lives. I want that too but I'm just so damn angry."

"At what?"

"Whoever did this to us! I'm filled with rage toward the person who kidnapped me, who took me away from a sane, normal, happy family and dragged me into…"

Her expression closed up and he wondered about her childhood after she was taken from her family, about what she might have been through to put that bleak look in her eyes. "Into a world far removed from the safe, happy life I likely would have known as Charlotte McKinnon."

Someone had kidnapped her more than two decades before. He hadn't been so self-absorbed that he didn't know all about that. Who was it? he suddenly wondered. And had they paid for the crime that had devastated the lives of so many people?

For the first time since his release—hell, since the shock of his arrest three years ago—he found himself concerned about someone else's problems, found himself actually interested enough to want to solve the mystery.

He wasn't sure he wanted to care, but he had been a cop too long to turn it off completely.

"Any idea who kidnapped you?"

"Until six weeks ago I thought my mother was a woman named Brenda Golightly. She's all I can remember until I was taken away from her and put into foster care when I was seven."

"And you think she was the one?"

"She must have been. My earliest memories are of her—driving beside her along a lonely stretch of highway. Sleeping in some dingy motel somewhere. Eating peanut-butter sandwiches and washing them down with warm soda. She's the one listed on all my records as my mother. I have a birth certificate and everything. I don't know how she did it but my name was Katie Golightly until I changed it at eighteen to Kate Spencer."

At least she had a name. He could work with a name. "Any idea where she is?"

"We don't exactly exchange Christmas cards. Brenda was a prostitute and a junkie, stoned more often than she was sober. After I was taken from her, she used to write or phone me once in a while but by the time I was in high school, she seemed to have lost interest—the letters and calls had trickled down to maybe once every couple of years. I was glad she didn't seem to want much to do with me. It was easier that way."

She paused, and again he wondered what dark images she was seeing in her memory.

"Anyway," Kate went on, "I haven't heard from her in nine years, since I left for college, but last I knew she was living in Miami somewhere."

He could drive to Florida in two days if he pushed it. The thought sneaked into his mind and Hunter drew in a sharp breath. Now who was the crazy one, contemplating a drive across the country on what was probably a fool's errand?

On the other hand, he didn't have anything else to do right now. He was restless and edgy and a road trip might be just the thing to help him figure out what to do with himself.

"Either she kidnapped me herself," Kate went on, "or she had to know who did it. I only want to know why. Why me?"

He studied her there in the moonlight, this small, beautiful woman with shadows in her eyes. He could help her. Like she said, he'd been a damn good detective once. Maybe he could be again. He had considered going into private-investigator work, the logical second career for a burned-out cop. This could be a way to test if he had the temperament for it.

One of them at least ought to be able to put some ghosts aside and move on. With a sneaking suspicion that he was going to have some serious regrets later about ever opening his mouth, he took the plunge.

"You want to know why you were taken," he finally said. "Why don't I find this Brenda Golightly and ask her?"

Chapter 2

Kate stared at him. He looked perfectly rational, his eyes dark and intense as he stood there in the cold night air with the soft snow sifting down around him like powdered sugar. But looks could be deceiving, she thought.

"Didn't you hear what I said? She's probably in Florida! The last address I had was Dade County."

"Sunshine sounds nice right about now."

No wonder, she thought. Since his release, sunny days had been few and far between in Utah. The state had seen a wet, cold fall—a boon for the ski resorts but probably not so enjoyable for someone who had been incarcerated for more than two years.

She had to admit, though she had grown to love the Utah mountains, the first place she would head if she had just been released from prison would be somewhere with an ocean view. Somewhere she could bask in the sun and lick salt from the air and dig her toes into warm sand.

But how could she ask him to travel across the country for her on little more than a whim?

"I haven't heard from Brenda in nearly a decade," she said. "She might not even be in Florida anymore. Heavens, for all I know, the woman could be dead."

"Then I'll find out where she's gone. Or at least where she's buried."

He said the words with complete confidence. She would have thought it an idle boast if he hadn't been such an outstanding detective. But if Hunter Bradshaw put his mind and energy into finding someone, he would. He had been dogged about his job, completely focused on it.

She had so many unanswered questions. Since finding out she had been kidnapped, her mind seemed to be racing on an endless loop of them.

Why had she been taken? Not for ransom, certainly, since the McKinnons said no one ever contacted them. And why *her?* What about Kate had made her a target of the kidnapping?

If Brenda had taken her, why had she then just surrendered Kate to the foster-care system, keeping only enough contact to ensure that no one could adopt her?

Finding the answers to those pressing questions was tantalizing. But the idea of Hunter Bradshaw offering to help her baffled her.

She was nothing to him, only the roommate of his younger sister. She couldn't even say she was a friend. Before his arrest and imprisonment, he had always been distantly polite to her but never more than that. She had even wondered if he disliked her because he seemed to go out of his way to avoid situations where they might be alone.

Yet here he was offering to chase after her past.

"Why would you do this for me?" she asked.

"Why not?" Hunter asked. In the dim light, his eyes wore an inscrutable expression. "You deserve to know the truth. I know how frustrating unanswered questions can be, just as I know what it's like to be punished for someone else's sins. I'd like to help you find out why."

She wasn't sure why—perhaps something in those shadows in his eyes—but she sensed another reason, something deeper. "What else?"

Hunter turned away from her to lean his forearms on the deck railing and gaze out at the shadowy mountains.

"Because I can." His voice was low and without inflection but suddenly his offer of assistance made perfect sense. It had nothing to do with her at all, she realized, but with him and his new freedom.

He had spent nearly three years of his life behind bars, where his choices had been severely limited. Others told him what he could eat, where he could go, even how he could dress. What a heady sense of control he must find in the idea that he could pick up and drive across the country on a whim!

"I see," she murmured.

He slanted a look at her. "Do you?"

"You know, you could take a trip wherever you want without having the burden of tracking down a drug addict and a prostitute who could be anywhere."

"I've been at loose ends since my release. I could use a distraction. This is a good one."

"It might take weeks, Hunter. I can't ask you to give up so much of your time."

His shrug rippled the fabric of his well-cut suit. He had always been a good dresser, she remembered. Back when he was a detective, he always took care with his clothing.

Before his arrest, he would sometimes stop by Taylor's house after work for some reason or other. Even with his tie loose, a hint of dark shadow stubbling his jaw and his white shirt perhaps not as crisp and starched as it had likely been in the morning, he had been enough to make her mouth water. She had always thought Hunter Bradshaw was strong and masculine and gorgeous.

She wasn't sure which she preferred, that slightly rumpled end-of-day Hunter or this elegant man in evening wear.

"You didn't ask, I offered," he said in answer to her earlier comment. "Anyway, my time is my own now."

"So take a cruise around the world if you want to go somewhere!"

Kate knew that like his sister, Hunter didn't need to work. He could spend the rest of his life traveling the world if he wanted to. Both of them had fathoms-deep trust funds that would support them forever if they wanted to live lives of luxury and ease.

Their parents had come from old money, although like Taylor, Hunter had always shunned the accoutrements of wealth. He had become an underpaid Utah public servant and lived quietly here in the family ski cabin.

"Let me do this, Kate. You're looking for answers and I'm looking for something to fill all this free time I've suddenly got. Seems to me this is a good way for both of us to get something we want."

She looked inside the house and caught a glimpse of her family. Wyatt danced with their mother now, Lynn small and delicate next to his lean rangy height. Gage stood in one corner talking to Sam, with a tired-looking Anna in his arms.

A gust of wind blew across the deck, sending the fairy lights dancing, and Kate shivered.

She should be inside with her family. They would be

looking for her soon. But despite the cold out here and the snow that was swirling around a little harder, she dreaded returning to that happy, bright group inside. The joy that lit their eyes whenever they caught sight of her scraped along her spine like a chipped fingernail.

She couldn't be the daughter and sister the McKinnons wanted and her own failure to be open and relaxed around them sat heavy and thick in her chest.

Brenda Golightly had stolen twenty-three years of her life. She had taken so much from Kate—didn't the woman who had caused such horrible pain in so many lives deserve to pay for what she had done?

Perhaps if Kate could find answers to some of the questions that had haunted her for six weeks since learning her true identity, she might at last be free to accept the love and nurturing this family seemed painfully eager to shower on her.

Didn't she owe it to the McKinnons and to herself to try and reclaim some of what had been taken from her?

She blew out a resigned breath. "It won't be easy to find her," she warned. "She could be anywhere. Brenda was always good at slipping under the radar."

Hunter gazed at her for a moment, his expression unreadable, then he nodded, recognizing she had decided to let him help her.

"If you have a previous address for her, I can work with that. I can leave tomorrow and start digging. I should be able to call you with information by the end of next week."

She looked at him standing in shadow, then shifted her gaze to that bright, gleaming window again. Laughter and music spilled out into the night. Would it always be this way? Would she always be on the outside looking in, separated from her family by the walls a stranger had erected between them by snatching her away so long ago? Would she always be unable to let herself partake of the love the McKinnons so wanted to give her because of her anger and bitterness?

That restlessness prowled through her again, edgy and fretful, and she blew out a breath and turned to face Hunter again in the shadows.

"You won't need to call me to report your progress."

He frowned. "Why not? Don't you think you'll want to know how things are going."

"Absolutely. That's why I'm going with you."

His mind already busy mapping a route and making plans, Hunter barely heard her. When her words pushed their way through his crowded thoughts, shock just about sent him toppling over the deck railing. She wanted to go along? Yeah, right!

He would never have suggested helping her if he thought for one second it might involve spending time alone with Kate Spencer.

"Really, that's not necessary."

Not necessary and not at all appealing.

"It is to me. This woman stole my life. My identity, my family, everything. If you can find her, I believe I have the right to confront her to find out why."

Okay, he would give her that. If he had been in Kate's shoes, he would have moved heaven and earth to locate this woman who had wreaked such havoc in her life.

He understood her need for answers and her desire to be involved in finding those answers but he didn't think she quite comprehended the implications.

"If I were flying out there for a quick trip," he explained, "I would have no problem with you going along. But I won't be taking a plane. If I go, I'm driving."

For one thing, he couldn't leave Belle, especially with Tay and Wyatt leaving for their Cozumel honeymoon in the morning. Since his release, his Irish setter clung to his side like a mother hen watching her chick. Though normally calm and well-mannered, she turned into a nervous wreck if he left her alone for even a few hours.

He wouldn't put her through the stress of a lonely kennel for a week or two, nor was he willing to subject her to the trauma of putting her on an airplane. The one time he had taken her on a plane before his arrest, she'd been a quivering mess for a week afterward.

He had to admit, Belle was part of the reason behind his sudden desire to drive, but she was by no means the only reason. The thought of taking off across the wide expanse of the United States with the road in front of him and Utah in his rear view mirror seemed just the thing to shake this malaise he'd suffered from since his release.

Those months he had spent on death row sure his life would end there in that miserable prison, he used to dream about hopping on his Ducati and zooming off across the country. When he would lie awake at night in that thin, lumpy cot staring up at cement walls, he had grieved for the trips he had never found time to take, for the scenery he would never have the chance to savor.

The Ducati would have to wait since December wasn't the greatest time for a motorcycle trip—not to mention the minor little detail that he hadn't yet taught Belle how to hang on behind him. But he could enjoy a cross-country trip from inside the brand-new Jeep Grand Cherokee he'd bought just days before.

What better way to celebrate his newfound freedom than loading up his dog and trekking across the country—eating in greasy diners, blasting his favorite songs on the radio at top volume, outrunning his past with every white line passing under his tires.

He would have thought his announcement would be enough to dissuade her, but Kate didn't seem at all fazed by his declaration. "Driving is fine. I don't mind a road trip," she answered.

Damn. So much for his peaceful jaunt across the country.

"Don't you have to work?" he asked, not willing to give it up just yet. "I thought residents worked sixty hours a week without a day off."

The Christmas lights sparkled in her glossy hair as she shook her head. "I'm free until I start my new rotation on Christmas Day. That gives me two weeks of freedom. This is a perfect time for me to go. I should have thought of it myself."

Now what the hell was he supposed to do? He couldn't just come out and tell her she couldn't go. For one thing, he was oddly loathe to hurt her feelings. For another, from his admittedly limited experience with Kate, he knew she was enough like Taylor that she would push and poke at him until she pried out the reason he didn't want her along.

He was well and truly stuck. He should have kept his big mouth shut about the whole thing.

It would take them a bare minimum of two days to drive to Miami. Two days alone in a car with Kate Spencer. For a man who hadn't been sexually intimate in nearly three years, that prospect was guaranteed to be a recipe for disaster.

He couldn't do it. He couldn't sleep with his sister's best friend just to slake his hunger. If he did, he would be exactly the kind of beast he'd been trying to prove to the world— and himself—that he wasn't.

"Look, Kate—" he started to say, but his words were lost when the door opened and Lynn McKinnon walked out onto the deck, her lovely features concerned.

"There you are, Charlotte!" She winced and reached for Kate's arm. "I'm so sorry, Kate. I keep forgetting. It's just that I've thought of you as Charlotte for so long. But I'll get it, I promise."

"It's fine," Kate murmured. The animation of the last ten minutes was gone from her features as she gazed at the small, energetic woman who looked so much like her.

"You're going to catch your death out here! Is everything all right?"

"We were just enjoying the snowstorm."

"Your father is still waiting for his dance."

"Of course." Even in the pale light, Hunter thought her smile looked strained. "I just need a few more minutes of air, okay? And then I'll be in."

Lynn's mouth softened as she gazed at her daughter, and Hunter thought she would have reached up and grabbed the moon for Kate if she asked for it. "Take as much time as you need, darling. Sam will be there whenever you're ready."

Kate managed another smile before her mother slipped back inside, though Hunter was surprised to see a bleakness in her eyes.

He muttered a string of curses in his mind. He couldn't leave her here twiddling her thumbs while he went off dragon hunting. This was her *life*.

Of all the people at this wedding gig, he could certainly understand her need to take back some kind of control over the circumstances that had buffeted her for the last six weeks. If finding and confronting her kidnapper would help her achieve some measure of peace—would help her move

past her pain and be ready to accept the McKinnons' love—
how could he deny her that?

Surely he was tough enough to control himself around
her for a week.

"What time are we leaving?" she asked after Lynn closed
the door behind herself and returned to the festivities, leaving them once more in the still, quiet night.

"Early. I'll pick you up at eight. Does that work?"

"Perfectly."

Was it just his imagination or did the pinched look around
her mouth ease just a little?

"I can't tell you how grateful I am for this," she said.
"Going after Brenda is a brilliant idea."

"Let's see how brilliant you think it is after a week on
the road."

This had to be the craziest idea she had ever come up with.

Worse, even, than the time when they were second-year
med students and she and Taylor had tried to break into the
anatomy lab for a little extra study time working on their ca-
davers.

In the cold, pale light of a December morning, what had
seemed so logical the night before seemed shortsighted and
foolish when faced with the cold, hard reality of spending
at least a week in intimate quarters with Hunter Bradshaw.

Kate stood at the front window of the small second-floor
apartment she had moved into the month before, watching
for him to pull into the driveway below.

A quick glance at the clock on the microwave told her
that even if he was obsessively punctual, he wouldn't arrive
for at least ten minutes, but she couldn't seem to pry herself away from the window where she stood tracing the fil-
igreed frost collecting on the other side.

She hadn't slept well, with her nerves on edge and her mind racing. She had finally tired of her tossing and turning a few hours before dawn and had climbed out of bed to start preparing for the trip.

The few things she planned to take had been packed and waiting by the door for hours and she spent the rest of the morning wrapping her few Christmas presents and scrubbing her apartment. Since she barely spent any time at all here, she could find little to clean, but at least she wouldn't be coming home to a mess.

With all her preparations done, she had little else to do now but stand here at the window watching for him and panicking about the sheer insanity of this situation her impulsiveness had thrust her into.

Whatever had compelled her to insist on traipsing along with Hunter Bradshaw? In what feeble-minded moment would that ever seem like a good idea?

How could she ever have been stupid enough to think she could travel blithely across the country with him when simply finding herself in the same room with the man left her flustered and giddy?

He had always made her insides tremble and her heart rate accelerate. She had been friends with Taylor since their first semester of medical school, more than five years ago. She could still remember the first time she met her friend's older brother. She and Taylor had been cramming for finals their second semester and had decided to grab a midnight snack at their favorite all-night diner, a humble little place downtown that served divine mashed potatoes with thick, creamy gravy.

They had walked in and Kate had only a few seconds to register a gorgeous man sitting in a booth in the front window with a couple of uniformed cops when Taylor had let out a delighted laugh and dragged her over to meet the brother she often talked about.

She could still remember her first impression—that the two of them shared an obviously close, affectionate relationship completely foreign to someone who had never had siblings of her own, except in a few foster families where she had been barely tolerated.

Her second impression of Hunter Bradshaw had been far more elemental and astonishing—an intense physical awareness of him unlike anything she'd ever experienced. As she gazed into dark blue eyes while Taylor introduced them, her stomach did a long, slow roll and she felt as if something had just squeezed out every molecule of air in her lungs.

The off-duty uniform cops had been flirtatious and charming to a couple of weary young med students and had insisted she and Taylor join them. To her growing dismay, Kate found herself squeezed next to Hunter in the red vinyl booth.

Throughout the next hour she had been painfully aware of every movement he made—the way he leaned an elbow back on the seat cushion, how his mouth quirked up a little higher on one side than the other when he smiled, the way his dark hair curled just a little on the ends.

Her sudden absorption with him had been as unexpected as it was mortifying.

She had always considered herself rather cold when it came to the opposite sex. Men had never been a high priority in her life. Sometimes they hardly seemed worth the energy it took to cater to their egos and their self-absorption.

She thought perhaps she'd been passed over on the whole libido thing because most of the kisses she had experienced in her twenty-two years on the earth to that point had been pleasant, certainly, but nothing to write home about.

In that tired old diner looking out at neon gleaming in the wet street, with her pulse jumping every time Hunter's long legs would brush against hers under the table or his shoulder would bump her, Kate finally started to get an inkling what all the fuss was about.

Taylor often gave her a hard time because she rarely dated the same man more than a few times. She never told her friend this but she was always looking for that same crazy, exciting, terrifying breathlessness she experienced whenever Hunter was around.

Not that she ever did anything about it. How could she? When she first met Hunter, he had just started dating Dru Ferrin, the ambitious, talented crime reporter at a local television station.

A few months later, Dru had announced she was pregnant and Hunter had become totally absorbed in trying to convince Dru to marry him, in the prospect of becoming a father.

Or so he thought, anyway. After Dru and her terminally ill mother were murdered, DNA tests proved Hunter had not fathered the eight-month-old fetus that had also died from his mother's gunshot wound.

She had grieved right along with him, first at the child's death then when he found out Dru had lied to him throughout her pregnancy. And then had come the horror of his arrest and the subsequent trial and wrongful conviction.

She had had a major crush on him. The knowledge mortified her. She was a doctor, for heaven's sake. Twenty-six years old, well on her way to being established in her chosen career path, and she had a crush on a sexy, dangerous, unreachable male as if she were thirteen years old fantasizing about a pop star.

How on earth would she keep her silly feelings to herself for a week or longer when it would be just the two of them alone on the road?

She would just have to do her best to treat him like she did male colleagues and her other male friends—casual and cheerfully friendly.

Could she pull it off? She was still trying to figure that out when she saw an SUV turn into the small parking area behind her battered six-year-old Honda.

As usual, her stomach performed a long, slow tremble at the sight of that muscular body climbing out of a gleaming Jeep Grand Cherokee the color of a mountain forest.

He wore jeans and a suede jacket that did nothing to hide his powerful build. His years in prison had turned what had already been a sexy, muscled build into something potent and dangerous.

Kate huffed out a breath, heat crawling across her cheeks. Not the kind of thing she should be noticing. She would never survive riding in such close quarters with him if she couldn't shove those kinds of thoughts completely out of her head.

She was a doctor who had seen more than her share of men's bodies, both muscled and otherwise. It might require a great deal of effort on her part but she needed to treat Hunter Bradshaw with the same courteous, impersonal distance she treated her patients.

The man was doing her a huge favor by helping her trace her past. The last thing he probably wanted was for her to go all gooey over him.

The doorbell chimed through her apartment and Kate pressed a hand to her stomach, where a whole brigade of butterflies were doing their thing.

After a few deep, cleansing breaths, she pasted on a polite smile and opened the door.

"Good morning," she said.

He returned her attempt at a smile with one of those shuttered looks he excelled at and she could feel more heat crawl across her cheeks.

"I'm all ready." She gestured to the few bags by the door—one suitcase, her laptop case and the emergency medical kit she always carried with her.

He blinked a few times at her meager luggage. "This is all you're taking? We might be gone a while."

"I don't need much. A few pairs of jeans and a toothbrush and I'm set."

He looked even more surprised by that piece of information. She wondered why, until she remembered his most recent experience with females, not counting his sister, had been Dru Ferrin—a girlie-girl if Kate had ever met one.

Dru probably wouldn't even have driven to the all-night grocery store at 3:00 a.m. unless she'd worn full battle armor. Kate doubted if Dru Ferrin could have gone anywhere without a footlocker full of makeup.

As soon as the thought flitted across her mind, she felt small and catty. She hadn't much liked Dru Ferrin, but the woman had died a horrible death. She deserved better than to be the object of malicious spite, simply because Kate was jealous that Hunter had loved her.

She made a face at herself and her own small-mindedness but Hunter must have misinterpreted the reason behind it.

"Are you sure you want to do this?" he asked quickly. "I can go by myself. It's not too late if you want to back out."

For just one moment she was tempted—horribly tempted—to do just that, especially when a hint of his aftershave wafted to her. He smelled divine, something leathery and outdoorsy and male, and for a moment she wanted to stand right here in her tiny living room just sniffing him.

She could handle this. Yes, she was attracted to the man but that was nothing new. She'd been dealing with that for five years now and had never done anything about it. A few more days wouldn't make much difference in the scheme of things, especially if she could keep the purpose for the whole trip uppermost in her mind.

"I need to do this, Hunter. I realized during the night that I have to try to make some kind of peace with my past. I can't spend the rest of my life being eaten alive by my anger."

"You think finding the woman you thought was your mother will help you find that peace?"

"I can only hope. I won't know for sure until I find her, will I?"

He studied her for a moment then shrugged. "Let's go, then."

He reached down and picked up her luggage effortlessly, then headed back down the stairs.

With an odd, tingly feeling in her toes like she teetered on the brink of something precarious and shaky, Kate made one last check of her apartment to ensure she had turned everything off, grabbed her coat, then locked the door behind her and followed him down the stairs.

Chapter 3

Hunter was stowing her suitcase in the cargo area of his new SUV next to Belle's travel crate when Kate walked down the steps of the old Victorian that had been split into three or four apartments.

"All set," she said. "Everything's turned off and locked tight."

He wondered if she realized her chipper tone seemed as forced as her smile—and about as enthusiastic as he felt about this whole thing.

Was she as apprehensive as he was about this whole road trip? He ought just to back out right now, let her fly down to Florida by herself on this quest of hers.

He couldn't do that, though. If he hadn't opened his big mouth and suggested it, she wouldn't even have grabbed onto the idea.

No, he had started this and he would see it through. He

had offered to help her, had made a commitment, and he was a man who honored his promises, no matter how difficult.

How tough could it be anyway? All he had to remember was that those columbine-blue eyes and that honey-blond hair and those lush delectable lips were off-limits. No worries.

To his surprise, Kate immediately opened the back door of the Jeep to greet Belle.

His setter barked in greeting and jumped from the vehicle, writhing around Kate with her tail wagging like crazy. Hunter was about to apologize and order Belle to settle down but before he could, Kate knelt down and wrapped her arms around the dog's neck.

"Oh, I've missed you, sweetie. How've you been?"

She didn't seem to mind Belle's slobbery greeting or the dog's enthusiastic licking of her face, or the hair she was undoubtedly depositing on Kate's gray sweater.

He supposed he shouldn't have been surprised by their happy reunion. While he had been locked up, Belle had lived with his sister and her roommate and best friend. Kate.

In truth, Belle had probably spent more time with Kate than she had with him. She was really more theirs than his. Belle had only been a few years old at the time he had been arrested.

His dog certainly hadn't suffered at all under their care. By the looks of things, the Irish setter adored Kate as much as him.

He let Belle work out a little of her energy by dancing around Kate a few times, then opened the door of her crate.

"Belle. Kennel."

With one last enthusiastic lick of Kate's hand, the dog leaped into her travel crate and settled in.

"It's safer for her to ride back here," he explained. "For

her sake and for the driver's. Belle's a good traveler but she can be a distraction."

"I know. Once she tried to attack the rear windshield wiper in Taylor's Subaru—from the inside of the vehicle, of course. She spent about ten minutes trying to figure out why she couldn't wrap her teeth around the thing."

Her smile looked more natural, a little less forced, and he had forced himself to look away, focusing instead on the clouds hanging heavy and dark in the December sky.

"We'd better get going," he said brusquely.

"Right," she said after an awkward moment, then headed for the passenger door of the SUV.

He beat her to it and held it open for her, earning himself an odd look, as if she weren't quite sure how to react to that small courtesy.

As he walked around the Jeep, he couldn't help thinking about the somewhat old-fashioned lessons his father had constantly drilled into his head about how to treat a woman. With respect and civility and basic human courtesy.

He and his father had certainly had their differences but he could never fault the Judge in that regard. His father's example had been lesson enough. Even when his mother had been at her most difficult—days when she had been barely coherent and had raged at everything in sight—Hunter never saw his father treat her with anything but dignity.

He doubted the Judge would find anything courteous about the thoughts he was entertaining about this particular woman. Like how the ivory December morning light gave her skin the soft delectability of a bowl of fresh apricots and how that full mouth begged to be devoured.

He paused outside the driver's side for one more last-minute lecture to himself. He had to send those kinds of thoughts right out of his head.

Okay, so he'd been a long time without a woman. He could have remedied that anytime these last six weeks if he'd chosen, but he hadn't and now it was too late. It was his own damn fault if he found himself in a near-constant state of arousal for the next few days.

With a heavy sigh, he opened the driver's side door and immediately wished he hadn't. He felt invaded. Overwhelmed. Instead of the comfortably male scent of leather and new car he expected, he smelled *Kate*—that subtle, alluring scent of shampoo and woman and the vanilla sugar that always clung to her. The smell seemed to slide over him like silk and he wanted to close his eyes and sink into it.

He gritted his teeth and climbed into the SUV.

They drove in silence for a block or so before he dared unclench his teeth to speak. "Your apartment seems comfortable."

She looked a little nonplussed by his comment coming out of nowhere. Okay, so he was a little rusty at making small talk. His companions for the past two years had been the other inmates on death row, who weren't exactly big on social chitchat. He was going to have to work on it, though, or this trip with Kate would be excruciating.

"Thanks," she said after a moment. "I had to find something in a hurry and this was one of the first places I looked at. I thought it was a graceful old house and I liked the fact that it was an established neighborhood. That was one of the things I enjoyed most about sharing Taylor's house in the Avenues, having neighbors who actually knew your name."

Guilt pinched at him and he felt like he had shoved her out onto the street. "You had to find somewhere else in a hurry because of me, right? I'm sorry about that."

"I'm not. You were coming home and that was the important thing. Anyway, the house in Little Cottonwood Can-

yon was yours. Taylor and I were only staying there tempo-
rarily after her cottage burned."

"After it was torched, you mean."

Her mouth tightened at the reminder. "Right. I was always planning on finding somewhere else. You and Taylor
deserved some time alone without me hanging around."

"You could have stayed. There was plenty of room."

She laughed a little. "Right. The roommate who would
never leave. That's me. Don't worry about me, Hunter. I like
my new place, even if I don't expect to be there long. I only
signed a six-month lease—I imagine when my residency is
over and I start my own family-medicine practice somewhere, I'll buy a house somewhere."

Her words reminded him of his own aimlessness since
his release. He needed to give some serious thought to what
he was going to do with the rest of his life, now that it had
been handed back to him. Maybe with the open road stretching out ahead of him, he might find inspiration.

"I do like my apartment," Kate went on, "but this is the
first time I've ever lived alone and I have to admit I'm finding it a little odd."

"You've always had roommates?" There. That sounded
just right. Casual and interested but not too inquisitive. They
were almost having a normal conversation.

She nodded. "I've been a struggling med student, remember? I found it hard enough to make ends meet. Sharing the rent helped ease the financial strain a little."

She lifted one shoulder. "Maybe by my second or third
year I would have decided I'd had enough of roommates and
moved out on my own but then Taylor bought her house and
asked me if I wanted to share it. I couldn't say no."

Hunter had to admit, that decision of his sister's to take
on a roommate had come as a surprise to him. Taylor had

bought her little cottage in the Avenues outright with her inheritance from their father. She certainly hadn't needed a roommate to share expenses but she had taken one anyway for the company.

Taylor wasn't like him in that respect, he reminded himself. He had never been much of a pack animal, but his sister loved having people around her. He knew she had been lonely those first few months after she'd bought her house and she'd been eager for Kate to move in.

Kate seemed to be waiting for him to respond, so he fished around in his mind until he found an appropriate question. "So do you miss having a roommate?"

She gazed out the windshield, at the minimal Sunday-morning traffic, then finally looked back at him. "I miss Taylor," she admitted. "That sounds silly, I know, but she was more than just a roommate. She was my best friend. The closest thing I had to a sister."

"You'll still be close."

"It's not going to be the same. I understand that. Don't get me wrong, I'm thrilled for her and Wyatt. They're perfect for each other, I could see that right away."

"Your brother is a good man."

"I know. Wyatt is strong and smart and funny. Just the kind of man Taylor needs."

What kind of man do you need? he almost asked but stopped himself just in time. None of his business. That kind of question would lead their fledgling conversation in a direction he absolutely didn't want it to go.

"He makes her happy," she said. "When it comes down to it, that's all that matters."

"Right," he murmured. He had to admit, he enjoyed seeing Taylor find some happiness. She deserved it. Both she and Wyatt did.

If not for the efforts of his sister and of Wyatt McKinnon, he would still be in that prison, feeling his soul shrivel more each day. Taylor had worked tirelessly to free him. She had put her dream of becoming a doctor like Kate on hold, switching instead to law school so she could fight for his appeal. Taylor had finally enlisted the help of Wyatt, who had been writing a book about Hunter's case.

In the process of trying to free him, she had been threatened, her house set ablaze, and finally had faced down death for his cause. He hadn't wanted her to sacrifice her dreams for him—or, heaven forbid, her life—and Hunter knew he could never repay his sister for all that she had done.

He supposed that was another of the reasons he was driving through the sparse Sunday-morning traffic heading south on I-15. He owed Taylor and Wyatt everything for all they had risked. Maybe by turning around and helping Kate—someone both of them cared about—he could start to check off a little of that debt.

"You're not taking I-80?" Kate asked as he passed the interchange—the Spaghetti Bowl, as the locals called it, for the various lanes twisting off in every direction like pasta in a dish.

He shook his head. "The weather report said that light snow we had last night gathered strength as it headed east and was due to hit Wyoming with a vengeance today. I figured if we head south now, down through Albuquerque and Amarillo, we'll escape the worst of it."

"Good thinking."

They encountered no delays traveling south across the Salt Lake Valley and, all too soon, they reached Bluffdale where the Point of the Mountain state prison sprawled out to the west of the highway, its buildings squat and depressing.

This was the first time he'd been this way since his release, Hunter realized. Perhaps he had made a point of staying north of the area without even realizing it.

If he had come this way before, he might have been prepared for the rush of anger and hatred rising like bile in his throat.

His hands tightened on the steering wheel. Sunday mornings were relatively quiet at the prison. Many prisoners chose to sleep the day away, while others attended the various religious services offered.

Hunter had quite deliberately chosen to stay in his cell reading. By the time he'd found himself on death row, he had lost whatever faith might have lingered in his soul.

He had been less than nothing in prison. Inhuman, like a dog locked up in a cage at the pound. He had been out for six weeks and he wondered if that feeling would ever go away.

"It's hard for you to see the prison, isn't it?"

It seemed a sign of weakness to admit the truth. It was just a cluster of buildings, after all. A part of his life that was over forever.

He opened his mouth to deny he was at all affected by the sight but somehow the lie caught in his throat.

"I lost two and a half years of my life to that bastard Martin James. Three lives were lost while he tried to protect his web of lies and deceit. Who knows how many more he would have taken? It's a little hard to get past that."

Her blue eyes softened with understanding and she reached a hand across the width of the SUV and touched his arm with gentle fingers. "I'm so sorry, Hunter."

Despite his grim thoughts, heat scorched him where she touched his arm and he was suddenly aware of a wild, terrible hunger to drown in that heat and softness, to lose some of this rage always seething just under the surface.

He jerked his arm away, just firmly enough to be obvious. "I'm sorry enough for myself. I don't need your pity, too."

She paled as if he had slapped her—which he guessed he had done, verbally at least—and quickly pulled her hand away.

"Right. Of course you don't."

He opened his mouth to apologize for his rudeness, then closed it again. Maybe it was better this way. They weren't buddies. It was going to be tough enough for him to stay away from her on this journey without having to endure shared confidences and these casual touches that would destroy him.

He had been without any kind of physical affection since his arrest and he hungered for gentleness and softness as much as for sex.

It was a grim realization, one that certainly didn't make their situation any easier.

She had two choices here, Kate thought as his blatant rejection burned through her like hydrochloric acid. She could let herself be hurt and pout for the rest of the day. That was the course that appealed to her most, but what would that accomplish?

Yes, her feelings had been hurt. All she had been trying to do was offer comfort and he had slapped her down like she was one of those inflatable punching bags she used to beat the heck out of when she was in foster care, angry at the world and unsure of her place in it.

But she decided not to let herself be offended. Hunter was a proud man who had seen his entire world crash down around him. He had lost friends, his job, his standing in the community.

It must have been agony for him to know the whole world believed him capable of murdering a pregnant woman and her dying mother.

He had a right to be prickly about it, to deal with his wrongful conviction and everything else that had happened in his own way. If that way included being surly and hostile when an unsuspecting soul tried to offer comfort, she couldn't blame him.

His bitterness and anger must be eating him up from the inside and she could certainly understand all about that.

She would take the higher road, she decided. Instead of snapping back or sulking all day, she would swallow her hurt feelings and pretend nothing had happened.

She decided a change of subject was in order. "I brought music if you're interested," she said, then risked a joke. "I figured your CD collection might be a few years out of date."

He sent her one of those dark, inscrutable looks she could only imagine must have been torture for any crime suspect he was questioning. He said nothing, but she thought she registered a vague surprise in those dark-blue eyes at her mild reaction to his rudeness, and she was immensely grateful she hadn't gone with her first instincts and thrown a hissy fit.

"What are you in the mood for?" she asked. "Jazz? Rock? Country? Christmas music? I've got a little of everything."

"I don't care. Anything."

"Okay. I'll pick first and then you can find something."

She chose Norah Jones and felt her own stress level immediately lower as soon as the music started.

They drove without speaking for several moments, Belle's snoring in the back and the peaceful music the only sound in the vehicle, then Kate reached into her bag again and pulled out Wyatt's latest bestseller that had come out a few months earlier.

"You don't mind if I read, do you?"

"Go ahead. We've got a long drive ahead of us. I imagine we're going to run out of small talk by the time we hit Spanish Fork."

She laughed. "*You* might. I never seem to run out of things to say. But I'll take pity on you and pace myself."

To her delight, that earned her a tiny, reluctant smile, but it was more than she'd seen since his release. It was a start, she thought. Maybe by the time this journey was through, he would be smiling and laughing like the man she had met five years ago with Taylor in that all-night diner.

She picked up her book, one of only a few of Wyatt's she hadn't had time to read yet. She had actually discovered his books long before she ever knew he was her brother, and had read each one with fascination.

He wrote true-crime books—usually not one of her favorite genres—but Wyatt had a way of crawling inside the heads of both the victims and the killers he wrote about, and she found his work absorbing and compelling.

This one was no different, and she was surprised by the warm contentment stealing over her as she rode along with Hunter's sexy male scent drifting around her senses and the tires spinning on the highway while the windshield wipers beat back a light snow spitting from the sky.

Combined with the peaceful music, Kate felt herself begin to relax and slip further into that warm, cozy place where she didn't have to worry about the family waiting patiently for her love—or the man beside her who wouldn't want it, if he ever guessed it might be his for the taking.

She must have drifted off to sleep. One moment she was reading the introduction to Wyatt's book, the next she woke facing Hunter, with her left cheek squished into the leather seat.

She blinked, disoriented for a moment, then whispered a fervent prayer that she hadn't done something humiliating in front of the man, like snore or drool or—heaven forbid—talk in her sleep.

They had stopped moving, she realized. The cessation of movement must have been what awakened her. The SUV was parked at the gas pump of a dusty, dilapidated filling station, far from the traffic and houses of the Wasatch Front.

"Where are we?" she asked, her voice gruff with sleep.

"A ways past Price. Sorry to wake you but Belle needed to get out."

"No. It's fine. I can't believe I fell asleep."

"Don't worry about it. You looked comfortable so I figured you needed it. I know what kind of hours you M.D.s keep." He started to say something more but Belle's sharp, impatient bark cut him off.

Kate winced. "That sounds urgent bordering on desperate. Why don't I go to that park across the street and play with her for a few moments while you fill up?" she offered.

"Thanks. I brought along a ball and a Frisbee. She likes either one." He looked a little embarrassed. "But I guess you know what she prefers, don't you? Probably better than I do."

That bitterness tinged his voice again and again she had to fight her instinctive urge to offer comfort.

He opened his car door and she caught sight of the gas pump again, which reminded her of something she meant to bring up earlier in the trip. She reached for the huge, slouchy purse she'd bought in Guatemala when she was there on a medical mission a few months earlier, and dug through it until she found her wallet.

She pulled out a credit card and handed it to him. "Use this for the gas."

With one hand on the frame of the SUV and the other on the door, he gazed at her, another of those unreadable expressions on his face. His mouth quirked a little as if he wanted to say something but he just shook his head.

"No," he said, and shut the door in her face.

Undeterred, she climbed out after him before he could come around and open her door. A cold wind nipped at her and lifted the ends of her hair. The air felt heavy, she thought. Moist and expectant, as if just waiting for the right moment to let loose. Maybe they wouldn't be able to skirt around the snowstorm after all.

She shoved away inane thoughts of the weather and focused on what was important. With her Visa tight in her hand, she marched to the rear door of the Grand Cherokee, where he stood hooking on Belle's leash so he could let her out of the crate.

"I mean it, Hunter. The only reason you're even here at some armpit of a gas station in the middle of nowhere is because of me. I intend to take care of expenses on this trip."

"I'm here because I want to be here," he corrected her. "It was my idea to go after the woman you're looking for."

"Right. The woman *I'm* looking for. That's my point. For all intents and purposes, you're my private investigator. You're working for me, so I should be footing the bill along the way."

He paused at that, his hands on Belle's crate as he closed the door. "Let's get one thing straight. I'm not working for you. I'm doing this because I want to do it, because I was looking for something to occupy my time, and because I need to be doing something useful."

"And I appreciate all those reasons. Believe me, I do. But you're still here because of me."

He sighed at her obstinate tone. "Look, I can afford it, okay?"

She lifted her chin. "So can I." So she had a pitiful resident's salary with medical-school debts that would probably take her the rest of her natural life to repay.

"Anyway, that's not the point," she went on, thrusting the card out to him again. "You're already going to have to give up a couple weeks out of your life on this quest. Please let me pay for expenses."

Belle chose that moment to break in, a slightly frantic note to her bark this time. Hunter let her jump from the vehicle, where she danced around them, eager to be off.

"You'd better take her," Hunter said, holding out the leash.

"Okay, as long as you take this."

She didn't wait for an answer—as she reached to accept the leash, she handed the Visa to him in return. With a victorious laugh, she hurried away after Belle, certain she was leaving him glaring after her.

Chapter 4

By the time he finished pumping gas into his Jeep, that cold, damp wind seemed to have picked up and a few stray snowflakes drifted down.

Hunter looked up at the heavy gray sky. The weather forecasters said the storm wasn't supposed to hit this part of the state, but it sure looked to him like those black-edged clouds were boiling around up there, ready to blow.

Maybe they could still outrun it before the center of the storm passed over. If the storm was heading east, as most low-pressure systems moved here in the Intermountain West, it might clip past them.

He might still have to drive through a little snow, but by the time they hit southern Utah in a few hours, it would probably be mostly rain.

Anyway, he didn't mind snow. He had spent his youth

driving the canyons of the Wasatch Front, skis strapped to the roof, looking for fresh powder.

When he was a kid, skiing had been his passion. He'd even been on the junior U.S. ski team for a while.

For the adult in him, skiing had been therapy. When he was stressed over a case and couldn't quite find the answer to whatever puzzle he was working on, he would take a few hours of personal leave and head for the slopes. More often than not, while his body focused on turns and terrain, his mind was able to come up with an answer.

He was chagrined to realize that even though most of the ski resorts had been open since mid-November, he hadn't been able to summon the energy to go yet.

The nozzle clicked off, signaling the tank was full. With a sigh, Hunter tightened the gas cap, then went inside to pay.

On the way, he pulled Taylor's credit card out of the pocket of his jacket and shoved it in his wallet before pulling out one of his own, new since his release and still shiny enough that the gilding on the numbers hadn't worn off.

He had absolutely no intention of letting Kate foot the bill for this trip. He meant what he'd said to her—this whole thing was his idea. He would pay his own way.

He decided he wouldn't make a big deal about it, though. He would just keep her card in his wallet until the trip was over, then give it back to her. He wasn't prepared for another confrontation with her, not when it made her eyes look bright and vibrant and gave her skin that appealing flush, raising all kinds of questions in his vivid imagination, like if she would look like that in his arms.

Inside the convenience store, he grabbed some liquid caffeine from the soda dispenser. He probably should have asked Kate if she wanted something, but he hadn't thought of it and he didn't have the first idea about her beverage preferences.

Being forced to consider someone else's likes and dislikes was a novel experience. Or at least not something he had considered much since his arrest three years earlier.

That was one of the unfortunate side effects of prison—behind bars, the world condensed to one of survival, to thinking of self before anything else.

At least for him it had. He knew men with families on the outside could spend their time thinking about them. He hadn't had anyone but Taylor. Though he worried about her, in his heart he had known she could take care of herself, as she had proved so adroitly a few months earlier.

It would take him a while to get into the rhythm of having someone else to consider.

He paid for the gas and his drink then carried it outside. He moved the Jeep so someone else could use the pump, and a few moments later he walked across the street to the park, where he could see Belle still gleefully chasing after a ball.

Without direct sunlight, colors were saturated in the overcast sky. The russet, sleek dog and Kate with her bright blond hair and gray sweater looked vibrant and alive playing in the light snow covering the ground.

Even from a hundred yards away, he could see Kate's smile light up her face as she watched Belle scramble through the snow after that ball as if it were made of raw hamburger.

She was breathtaking in that pale light, like something out of an impressionist painting.

He had always been attracted to Kate, he acknowledged now. He had never done anything about it, in fact he had gone out of his way to avoid situations like this one where they would be alone.

He *couldn't* do anything about it. For one thing, she was Taylor's closest friend. His sister hadn't had all that many close friends and he wasn't about to screw this up for her by messing around with Kate.

He had a poor history with women. Until Dru, most of his relationships had ended after only a few months, usually because the women he dated tired quickly of his complete dedication to his job. Dru hadn't minded; in fact she had encouraged him to talk about work. In retrospect, he wondered how much of that was genuine interest and how much was her reporter instincts, nosing around for a good story.

He had a feeling their relationship would have gone the way of all those others if she hadn't told him after only a few months of dating that she was pregnant.

Since her murder, he'd had plenty of time to think about things between them. He knew now that he had tried to convince himself he loved her because he'd thought she was pregnant with his child and he'd wanted fiercely to make things work between them.

His son deserved a father and Hunter intended to be part of his life. The best way to accomplish that—the right thing to do—was to marry his child's mother.

Dru had refused, though. Oh, she hadn't minded him taking her to doctor appointments and fussing over her, but she wasn't ready to marry him, she said. Now he knew the reason why. She had likely known—or at least suspected—that he wasn't her baby's father.

Kate's laughter rippled across the cold air suddenly, distracting him from the grim direction of his thoughts.

He could never act on this attraction simmering through him, he thought as he approached them. He didn't have room in his life right now for a woman and, even if he did, it wouldn't be this particular one.

"Hey." She greeted him with a smile. "I've almost worn her out. A few more throws and I think she'll be good for a while."

He held a hand out for the ball. When she gave it to him, he hurled it to the other side of the park.

"All right, show off." Kate laughed as Belle let out an ecstatic bark and set off after it. "Let me guess. You were a baseball player in another life."

He shrugged. "All-state in high school. When I wasn't skiing, I was throwing a ball through a tire hung up in the backyard. I played one year of college ball and had dreams of the majors, then I messed up my shoulder." Not that the Judge had ever encouraged those dreams for a second.

"So you decided to become a cop instead."

"Right." He didn't add that he had dreamed of being a cop as a boy but had entered the police academy mostly in an effort to piss off his father, who would see nothing else for his son except that Hunter should follow in his footsteps and study law.

To Hunter's surprise, he had thrived at the academy. By the time he'd graduated first in his class, he knew he had discovered his calling.

Or he thought he had, anyway. As much as he had loved being a cop, first on the beat then as a detective, he had been betrayed by the brotherhood. He couldn't work upholding a system he no longer respected.

"Do you miss it?"

He wasn't sure what to say, since the answer to that question was anything but an easy one. Did he miss it? Yeah. He'd been a good cop, a dedicated one. But he certainly didn't miss it enough to jump right back into the fray.

He was spared from having to answer by the return of Belle, who came panting back with the ball tightly clenched in her teeth. She rushed to Hunter and dropped the drooly thing like an offering at his feet.

"Good girl." He rewarded her with one of the treats he'd brought from the Jeep. She gulped it down then barked with joy when Hunter threw the ball hard for her again.

What was it about dogs? he wondered. They never seemed to get tired of the same activity. Give Belle a ball and a little attention and she was content for hours.

"Do you?" Kate asked again. He sighed. He hoped she would let the matter drop, but he supposed he wasn't really surprised when she didn't. The woman was nothing if not tenacious.

"Sometimes," he admitted. "I loved being a detective, helping people find justice. Giving them answers. The badge meant something to me." He gazed across the park at a pair of forlorn swings, chains rattling in the cold wind. "But I had already come to hate the politics of the job before I was arrested."

She nodded her understanding. "I suppose it's the same as medicine. I love treating patients but I can't stand dealing with insurance companies and HMOs. I guess it's true that sometimes you have to take the bad with the good."

"And sometimes it's easier to walk away from both."

She opened her mouth to argue but before she could say anything, Belle came bounding back with the ball. She came running at them just a little too fast, though, and bumped into Kate's legs in her rush to get to Hunter.

Kate wobbled a little and tried to keep her balance but the light layer of snow made gaining traction difficult. She gave a small cry as her legs started to slip out from under.

He didn't take time to think—if he had, he would have known reaching for her was a bad idea. Still, he couldn't let her fall.

He grabbed her to keep her upright, blocking her from falling with his own body. Her hands came out to grab something solid to hang onto—his shirt, as it turned out—and his arms came around her.

Though she was small, only five-four, maybe, she was sturdy. Still, she felt tiny and fragile in his arms.

"Are you all right?" he asked, his voice gruff.

"Yes. Yes, I think so."

Hunter wasn't. He felt frozen, cast in bronze like that statue in the corner of the park of a couple of soldiers crouched over what looked like a piece of World War II heavy artillery.

How long had it been since his arms had held a warm female? Forever. So long, he'd forgotten how absolutely perfect it could be to feel all those intriguing curves and angles, to be surrounded by the mouthwatering vanilla-sugar scent of her, to know he only had to bend his head down a little to capture that perfect, lush mouth for his own.

He had to let her go. The thought flickered through his mind then flew away like a killdeer on the side of the road.

Her eyes, wide and lovely in that delicate face, gazed up at him, full of confusion and embarrassment and what he thought might be sexual awareness—though it had been a hell of a long time since he had seen it, so maybe he was wrong about that last bit.

She made no effort to pull away. Instead her hands seemed to curl in his sweater and her dewy lips parted a little as she hitched in a ragged little breath.

They stood there, eyes locked and bodies entwined, as the moment seemed to drag on forever. He was vaguely aware of the cold seeping through his boots, of those swings creaking in the wind, of a pickup truck driving past. But nothing else mattered but this moment.

This woman.

He had to think he would have gotten around to letting her go eventually, but Belle took matters out of his hands. She whimpered as if she knew she'd messed up and nudged the back of his leg.

The contact seemed to jerk him back to his senses. What was he doing? In another second, he would have thrown caution to that cold wind and done exactly what his body was loudly urging him to do. He would have kissed Kate Spencer right here in a public park in Nowheresville, Utah.

And what a disaster that would have been!

Kate took a step backward quickly, and he was instantly cold, far colder than he should have been even with the chill wind.

"We should probably be on our way again," Kate murmured. Her voice sounded a little thready, a little breathless, as if she had just hiked the steep trail behind his family's ski cabin in Little Cottonwood Canyon.

"Yeah. You're right." He scrambled for something to say. Should he apologize? No, he hadn't done anything. Not really, only held her a moment—or two or three—longer than strictly necessary.

"I, uh, need to give Belle some water now. That will take me a few moments, if you need to make a trip inside the gas station."

She looked blank for a moment, as if she couldn't quite figure out why she might need to make a trip inside the gas station, then he saw understanding dawn in her eyes.

Despite his best intentions, he couldn't help being amused, charmed, by the color that spread across her elegant cheekbones.

She was a doctor who had undoubtedly seen things that would make his hair curl, but she could still blush at a suggestion that she might need to use the ladies' room.

"Right. Yes. I'll only be a moment."

They walked across the street together, then their paths diverged as he headed for the SUV and she went inside the gas station. He paused and watched until she went inside, reliving the heat and *rightness* of holding her in his arms for those few seconds.

If he responded so forcefully just to a platonic embrace, how the hell was he going to keep his hands off her this entire trip?

In the surprisingly clean restroom of the gas station, Kate stood at the sink for several moments, her cold hands covering the heat still soaking her cheeks.

She was such an idiot. She wanted to die, to sink through the floor—or at least to hide in this bathroom for the rest of her natural life.

What must he think of her? He had only been trying to keep her on her feet after that lovely show of grace and poise she had demonstrated. Just extending a courteous hand—like his habit of opening the door for her, keeping her upright had been only another polite gesture.

But the moment she found herself in such close contact, surrounded by those hard muscles and that rugged, masculine scent of him, she dug her hands into his sweater and held on for dear life.

And then she had made things worse by standing there, staring into his eyes, willing with all her heart for him to kiss her.

She fought the urge to bang her head against the mirror a few dozen times. She was an *idiot!* One who should certainly know better than to make mooneyes at a man who had no interest in her whatsoever.

Still, there had been a moment there when she thought

she saw something in those dark blue eyes. Something intense and glittering and just out of reach. And he hadn't exactly pushed her away, either, even after she regained her balance.

Why not? she wondered.

She certainly wasn't going to find any answers staring into the mirror of some convenience-store bathroom. If she didn't hurry, they would be on the road forever.

She blew out a breath, did her best without a comb to straighten the wind-tangles from her hair, then walked out into the convenience store.

By the time she bought a couple bottles of water, some power bars and deli sandwiches that looked surprisingly fresh for later, she had nearly regained her equilibrium. At least she felt a little more centered, almost in control.

At the Jeep, Kate found Belle in her crate and Hunter leaning against the vehicle gazing up at the dark clouds, his arms folded across his chest. He straightened at her approach.

"Sorry I took so long," she said, hating that breathless note in her voice. "I bought some provisions so we don't have to stop for lunch."

"Good idea." He moved around the vehicle to open the passenger door for her, which reminded her of something else she meant to bring up.

"Would you like me to drive for a while?" she asked.

He shook his head. "Maybe later. We've barely started."

She wanted to remind him not to overdo it, to pace himself, but she was afraid that would sound entirely too much like a nagging wife, so she held her tongue. Besides, she knew if she had just spent the last thirty months in prison, she wouldn't want to give up one iota of control to another person, in driving or anything else.

With her small bundle of provisions, she climbed into the passenger seat. He closed the door then walked around to the driver's side and a few moments later they were back on the road.

After they left the gas station, she tried a few times to make conversation, but gave up when his answers were short and choppy.

Fine, she thought. If the man wanted to ride three thousand miles as quiet as a post, she could entertain herself. She popped in a CD—a group she'd fallen in love with at the Snowbird Bluegrass Festival the summer before—kicked off her shoes, and pulled her book out again.

It was difficult to focus with Hunter sitting next to her but she called on the same powers of concentration that had helped her survive medical school and was soon lost in Wyatt's prose.

She wasn't sure how long she read, but she finally wrenched her attention away when her stomach growled again. If she wasn't mistaken, that was at least the second time through the CD. She knew one corner of her brain had registered hearing that song already.

She reached to stop the CD player. "Sorry. I'm afraid Wyatt sucked me right in."

He shifted his gaze briefly to her before returning his attention to the road stretching out ahead of them. "Yeah, your brother spins a good story, doesn't he? I read a few of his books in prison."

"Is that why you agreed to let him interview you?" Kate knew Wyatt was writing a book about the Ferrin murders. That was how he had met Taylor, the impetus behind the sequence of events that had led to Hunter's sentence being voided by the state supreme court.

"I knew someone would write about the case. It was sensational enough that I knew it was only a matter of time. I was impressed by McKinnon's writing and the way he treated the victims, with a dignity and respect that's missing in a lot of other books of that genre. That's why I agreed to cooperate with him instead of any of the other authors who contacted me."

What must it have been like for him, she wondered, knowing he was innocent but being bombarded by members of the media who all thought him guilty as sin?

"You know, it was odd," she said. "I don't normally pick up true-crime books for my leisure reading—when I have time for leisure reading, which isn't very often. But Wyatt's books really appealed to me, right from the first. I read nearly his entire backlist before I ever knew…"

She tightened her lips as her voice trailed off. Why could she never seem to squeeze those words out? They tangled in her throat, lodged there like she'd swallowed a rock.

To her relief, Hunter finished the sentence for her. "Before you knew he was your brother?"

"Right," she murmured.

She didn't know much about siblings but Wyatt and Gage certainly didn't feel like brothers. They were simply two very nice men who happened to share the same blood as her.

She admired them and enjoyed being in their company, but when she dug around in her heart for something deeper, she came up completely empty. Would that ever change? she wondered.

"What's this book about?"

She passed him a sandwich from her provisions and the bottled water, and outlined the case *Blood Feud* focused on and a few of the key players in it. While they ate lunch on the go, they spent several moments discussing other Wyatt McKinnon books they had each read. To her surprise, they actually were able to carry on an intelligent discussion. As a former homicide detective, Hunter had interesting insight about police procedure.

Fledgling hope stirred inside her. Perhaps this trip didn't have to be days of long, awkward silences after all.

"You certainly know enough about that world. Both sides of it, actually—the inside and the outside of the criminal justice system. Maybe *you* ought to write a book."

He stared at her for a moment, then he actually laughed. Kate almost couldn't believe it! It was short and abrupt, but was definitely genuine.

"I can't imagine anything more torturous. I'm no writer. It was all I could do to pass freshman English in college. Filling out my case paperwork was a nightmare."

"Well, you could always collaborate with Wyatt."

"Been there, done that. No thanks. After he finishes the book about Dru and Mickie's murders, I think my collaboration days are over forever."

"You don't want to go back to being a cop and you don't think you're cut out to be a writer. What will you do?"

He sent her a sidelong look over his sandwich. "I've been thinking. Maybe I'll just spend the rest of my life driving around the country helping damsels in distress."

Was that a joke? She stared at him, unable to believe her ears. Hunter Bradshaw actually made a joke!

"Interesting career choice," she murmured. "But I'm sure you can make a go of it. If you put out an ad, I'm sure you'll have distressed damsels crawling out of the woodwork."

Especially if you include a picture, one that shows your dark and dangerous side, she wanted to add, but didn't quite have the nerve.

"I'll be sure to include advertising in my business plan, then."

She smiled. "And if you need a reference, let me know."

"Better wait to see if we actually accomplish anything on this quest before you make an offer like that."

"We will. I have great faith in you."

"Good thing one of us does," he muttered, his features austere once more, with no trace of that fleeting lightheartedness.

Unsettled at his rapid transition, Kate turned to look out the window. They rode in silence for a few moments, but she thought it was a little more comfortable between them now.

Not *easy,* exactly, but getting there.

"I love this part of the state," she said after a few more miles. "The hoodoos and the mesas and the slickrock. It's like we're on another planet from the high mountain valleys of northern Utah."

"I haven't been this far south for probably five or six years. I'd forgotten how raw and primitively beautiful the desert can be in the winter."

"Taylor and I drove down to Moab to mountain bike a few times during med school."

"Really?"

"Why do you sound so surprised?"

"Every time I saw the two of you, you had your noses stuck in medical school textbooks. I wouldn't have thought you would make time for a vacation to shred up the slickrock."

"We weren't completely obsessed," she said with a laugh. "We took time away from studying when it was for something really important, like mountain biking."

"You've been a good friend to Taylor," he said after a moment.

"She's been good to me," Kate said simply. "I'm glad

she's going back to finish her last year of med school. It's been so wonderful these last few weeks to have the old Taylor back."

"What do you mean, *have her back?*"

She regretted her words as soon as she uttered them but it was too late to backpedal. She picked her next words more carefully. "You know how she's been since your arrest. She was driven before as a medical student—both of us were, that was the big link between us. But when she switched to law school to help with your appeal, Taylor went beyond driven."

"She was obsessed with the case. You don't have to sugarcoat it."

"*Obsessed* is a strong word and I'm not sure it's the right one, but she didn't allow much room in her life for anything else."

"For anything but trying to bail out her jailbird brother."

The bitterness in his eyes pierced her like a lancet. "No," she said firmly, earnestly. "Trying to right a terrible wrong. Trying to save the life of an innocent man."

He didn't say anything for a few more miles. She was just about to ask if he wanted to listen to another CD when he finally spoke.

"What about you?" He made his voice quiet, deceptively casual. "Did you think, like everyone else, that I was guilty as hell, that Taylor was wasting her time?"

"Never. Not for one single moment."

The vehemence in her voice stunned him enough that he shifted his gaze from the road to look at her. He saw no dissemination in her columbine-blue eyes, no hint of doubt. Only pure trust, absolute certainty.

He jerked his gaze back to the road, his mind barely registering the passing yellow lines under his tires. "How could you be so sure? You barely knew me. My closest brothers on the force thought I was guilty."

Men he had worked beside, would have taken a bullet for. Of all the crushing betrayals of the last thirty months, that had been the worst, that more police officers hadn't been willing to stand with him.

"They all thought I did it," he went on. "How could you be so sure I didn't?"

She paused so long he finally looked at her again. What had he said to put that light blush across her cheekbones? he wondered.

"I saw you with Dru," she murmured. "Even though you were angry that she refused to marry you after she found out she was pregnant, you still treated her like fragile, priceless glass."

"The prosecution would have said that was all the more reason for me to be furious when I found out she was cheating on me, when I found out the baby wasn't mine. All the more reason for me to kill her in a jealous rage—because I had been a blind, besotted fool."

"Whatever Dru did—no matter how she treated you— you never would have hurt her. And you absolutely would never have done anything to harm that baby. *Never.*"

That solid, unwavering faith shook him to his core, somehow managed to sneak under all those hard, crusty protective layers he had worked so hard to build these last thirty months. The cold, hard knot that had been tangled around his heart, his lungs, eased just a little and he almost thought he could breathe just a little easier.

Except for Taylor, he had felt completely alone in prison. Even Taylor's unwavering support had been small comfort, he was ashamed to admit. As his sister, she was supposed to believe in him. He had both needed and expected her faith in him.

Kate definitely wasn't his sister but she had believed in him, too. He shouldn't have found the knowledge so achingly sweet.

But he did.

Hunter was quiet for a long time after she uttered her fervent declaration, so long Kate wondered if she had embarrassed him by it.

Maybe she shouldn't have been quite so ardently enthusiastic in her support of him. She couldn't help it, though. She was so *angry* at what had been done to him, first by that bitch Dru Ferrin and then by the system of justice he had risked his life day after day to uphold.

The miles ticked by and for a long time she stared out the window watching dark clouds scud by above the desert, moving even faster than they were. Finally, she turned back to her book but she found it much harder to concentrate than she had earlier. She was relieved when Hunter stopped the SUV on the outskirts of Moab to fill up again and let Belle out.

Their first pit stop earlier in the day set the pattern for this one. Once more they worked as a team—Hunter pumped gas while she found an open space to exercise Belle for a few moments.

This time, though, when they finished she offered to drive again. To her surprise, he agreed.

The SUV handled even better than her little Honda, she was pleased to discover. Kate took off heading south while Hunter, big and rangy in the seat next to her, leafed through her CD collection for several moments.

She waited, curious as to what he might pick. Music was one of her passions and her collection was eclectic and extensive. Most men she dated tended to favor her blues or classic-rock CDs but she had to admit to some surprise at Hunter's ultimate choice—Dianne Reeves, one of her favorite jazz vocalists.

"I saw her in concert once at Red Butte," he explained at her raised eyebrow.

They listened in silence for a few moments while she adjusted her driving instincts to the SUV's bigger frame and longer braking time. By the third song, she glanced over and was further surprised to find Hunter's eyes closed.

At first she wondered if he might be feigning sleep to avoid making conversation, but after a few moments of the steady rise and fall of his chest, she was certain he was genuinely asleep.

This was nice, she thought. Driving along through harshly beautiful scenery with a gorgeous man sleeping in the seat beside her, while soft jazz kept her company.

Not a bad way to spend a Sunday afternoon at all.

Chapter 5

He was in heaven.

A paradise of sensations—heat and hunger and the sweet tug of anticipation.

He was lying on a beach, palm fronds rustling and clicking overhead. Sunlight seeped into his bare skin, his toes dug into warm sand and his arms were filled with naked womanly curves.

Heaven.

Kate.

She was everything he hadn't let himself imagine. Her skin was creamy and smooth and when he pressed his mouth to the curve of one shoulder, she tasted like sun-warmed vanilla candy. He wanted to lick every inch of it, to work his way from her pink-polished toes to that sweetly bowed mouth then back again.

"Mmmm, that's good," she murmured, arching her back

as she stretched beneath him so that the tight buds of her nipples brushed against the hard muscles of his chest.

He groaned and kissed her neck, that intriguing hollow just above her collarbone, then shifted his body just enough that he could cup one of those warm, tantalizing breasts in his fingers.

She made a soft, erotic sound and arched again, long, smooth legs sliding against his. She wrapped her arms around him, pulling him close.

He couldn't seem to breath as a torrent of sensations crashed over him like those sea waves buffeting the shore. So long. It had been so terribly long since he had tasted and touched and explored the mysteries of a woman's body.

She called his name and her low voice rippled down his spine like a slow, warm trickle of suntan lotion on his skin. He reached for her again, craving her touch with every cell, every synapse. She came to him with an eagerness that stunned and aroused him, with that secretive, seductive smile that hinted of female delights he had nearly forgotten.

"I want you," he murmured.

Her sleepy-lidded eyes beckoned him. "I know."

One hand slipped from behind his back between their bodies. He waited, stomach muscles contracted, not a single particle of air in his lungs, as she reached for him.

Her hand moved with agonizing slowness, down, down and it was all he could do not to whimper.

He had never been so aroused, never wanted so ferociously. He couldn't wait, he wanted to consume her. To take her until neither of them could move. Fast, slow, and every way in between.

"Hunter?"

The voice came again, more insistently this time. Instead

of a warm, sensuous whisper, this time it blew across his skin like the Arctic Ocean had suddenly come crashing over him.

In an instant, everything disappeared, yanked away with such cruel abruptness he wanted to bellow with rage. The warm sand, the sunshine, the naked and beautiful Kate in his arms. It was all gone.

He blinked quickly back to awareness, to the inside of his Jeep, to Belle snuffling around in her crate. Instead of warm tropical breezes, snow whirled around outside the SUV, blowing hard across the highway.

A dream. He was having a dream about Kate Spencer, about making love to her on some tropical beach, while she sat oblivious two feet away.

Holy hell.

He drew in a ragged breath, more grateful than he had ever been in his life that sometime while he'd slept she must have covered him with that fleece blanket he'd put behind the front seat in case of emergency.

This definitely qualified as an emergency. He was so aroused, it was a wonder he hadn't popped a few buttons on his Levi's.

He was sick thinking about what might have happened if she hadn't awakened him—and if the blanket wasn't hiding his obvious arousal. In another few moments, he would probably have embarrassed them both, something that hadn't happened to him since he'd hit puberty.

He would have had to move away, to another country, possibly another continent. Though he would have hated it, he would have had to break off all contact with his own sister to avoid ever having to see Kate again.

He had been far too long without intimacy. While on one level it was good to know he was still capable of all the normal hunger he thought had shriveled away during his incarceration, he would really rather not have discovered this salient fact on a long road trip with the one woman he couldn't have.

He could only hope and pray he hadn't said anything incriminating while he'd slept, that he had only done all that moaning and groaning in the feverish recesses of his mind.

Hunter blew out a breath and tried to focus on anything but the need still centered in his groin.

Even though the electronic clock on the dashboard read only five-thirty, the sky had darkened while he'd slept. They were approaching the shortest day of the year, he remembered. Outside the window, he saw nothing but snow swirling in their headlights. No house lights, no headlight beams from other traffic.

It was otherworldly, that total absence of life, as if they were completely alone in their own intimate little universe. His shoulder blades itched and he almost—not quite—forgot about that horrifying dream.

"Where are we?"

"On the Navajo Reservation. The last road sign said five miles to Shiprock, so we should be seeing some signs of life soon."

"How long has it been snowing?"

"Right before I hit Blanding."

That must have been a hundred miles ago! He couldn't believe he'd slept that long or that deeply. He couldn't remember the last time he'd slept three hours at a stretch.

Of course, he couldn't remember the last erotic dream he'd had, either.

His lingering embarrassment turned him surly. "I told you to wake me up if the weather turned bad. Why the hell didn't you do what I said?"

"There was no reason to wake you. I was doing fine. I'm still doing fine. You looked like you needed the rest and I didn't see any need to disturb you. I wouldn't have awakened you now except I thought since it's your vehicle here I'd better check to see if you want to stop in Shiprock and wait out the storm or keep driving onto Farmington or points south. I've been listening to weather reports on the one station I've been able to get and they're saying it's snowing hard between Farmington and Albuquerque and the Weather Service has issued a travel advisory."

Damn. So much for his plans to reach Albuquerque that night—or his hopes of outmaneuvering the storm by heading south. He had to hope this wasn't a grim precursor of what was to come on this trip.

"I guess we'd better stop in Shiprock for the night. Pull over and I'll drive from here."

She slanted him a quick, amused look before turning her attention back to the road. "Why? I'm perfectly comfortable driving in snow."

But *he* wasn't comfortable with her driving in snow. It was irrational, he knew, as from what he could see she was handling his SUV just fine.

She wasn't exactly driving at a snail's pace but her speed didn't seem at all excessive for conditions. She had engaged the on-demand four-wheel drive, he noted, and she seemed very competent behind the wheel.

She was a doctor. No doubt her hands were probably capable of all kinds of things.

The thought reminded him of that damn vivid dream, of those hands caressing him, reaching for him....

Hunter pushed the memory aside quickly.

"We should keep an eye out for a hotel, since it looks like we're starting to hit civilization."

They discovered as they drove slowly through town that Shiprock had very little in the way of overnight lodging. At last, almost at the outskirts, they stumbled past a small two-story hotel with a neon Vacancy sign out front. Underneath it was an even more encouraging message—Pets Welcome.

Kate pulled a U-turn in the deserted street. The Jeep slid a little as she made the turn but she expertly maneuvered out of the skid and pulled up in front of the modest brown brick building.

The parking lot was crowded with vehicles. His heart sank until he remembered that Vacancy sign out front.

"Wait here. I'll see what they have," Hunter said.

Kate nodded and he climbed out, relieved that any lingering effects from that dream had expired.

The lobby was pleasant but impersonal. The only bright spots were a striking woven Navajo rug hanging behind the front desk, a homely Christmas tree that looked like some kind of juniper gleaming cheerfully in one corner, and a sign that read Happy Holidays and what he assumed was the same sentiment in another language, undoubtedly Navajo.

The clerk was about forty with a round, cheerful face and smooth black hair that reached past her hips. She looked frazzled but still managed a smile as he approached the desk.

"You're in luck," she said in response to his request. "You'll be taking my last two rooms. Usually this time of year we're pretty empty but I guess you're not the only ones looking to get out of the snow today. Don't blame you a bit. Looks like a bad one out there."

He let out the breath he hadn't realized he'd been holding. At least they wouldn't have to share a room. He wasn't sure if his taut nerves could handle that. After nine hours in the car with her, he desperately craved a little distance to regain his much-needed control.

He handed over his credit card. As he waited for her to process it, his gaze shifted out the window. While he had been speaking to the clerk, another vehicle had pulled up behind his SUV and, out of habit, Hunter automatically catalogued the make and the model and the occupants—a woman and what looked like two small children, in a late-model extended-cab pickup truck with a sleeper shell, Utah plates.

The woman lumbered out and rocked her torso back and forth on her hips for a moment, her hands pressed to the small of her back. As soon as she turned, he realized why the need to stretch. She looked at least eight months pregnant and even from here he could see the fatigue and discomfort in her features.

She walked inside the hotel lobby shaking off the snow that had collected on her parka just in the short distance between her vehicle and the building.

The woman mustered a tired smile that didn't come close to reaching her eyes, the color of creamy hot cocoa. "*Ya'at eeh.* Your sign out front says Vacancy. I need a room for one adult and two children."

Any minute now, it looked like that tally would rise to three children, Hunter thought.

The clerk's hair rippled in a sleek black waterfall as she shook her head regretfully. "Haven't had time to turn off the sign yet. Sorry, but I just gave our last two rooms to this fellow here. You might try the SleepEasy, down at the other end of town."

Everything about the pregnant woman seemed to sag in defeat. "I just came from there. They were full, too. Guess we'll try to push on through to Farmington."

She looked as if she barely had the energy to walk back to her truck, forget about driving through a blizzard to the next town.

Hunter muttered an oath. He couldn't turn a pregnant woman and her children out into the teeth of a blizzard— even if his spontaneous act of generosity would mean he had to spend the night trapped in a room with Kate Spencer.

"Stop." The word burst out of him just as the woman reached the door. Damn, he was going to regret this. But he knew he would regret it even more if he let her walk out. "Look, we can get by with one room. You take the other one."

The woman turned, wary and hopeful at the same time, as if fate had handed her so many disappointments she was afraid to believe this chance wouldn't be snatched out of her hands.

"Are you…are you sure?"

"Yeah," he growled, though his mind was already filling with all kinds of forbidden images. Kate walking out of the shower, her hair damp and that beautiful face scrubbed clean. Kate curled up in the next bed. Kate waking up in the morning, all soft and warm and welcoming…

"Both rooms have two double beds," the clerk offered helpfully.

That was something, at least. If he had to share a room with Kate, he knew he would be up all night. But at least with two beds he could pretend to sleep on a bed instead of pretending to sleep on the floor.

He grabbed the two key envelopes the clerk had prepared and handed one to the woman. "Here you go."

"I can pay for it," she said, somewhat stiffly.

"The charge has already gone through on my card. It would be a hassle to void it, so don't worry about it."

"But…"

Something in his expression must have stopped her argument. Tears swelled in her eyes but to his relief they didn't spill out. She was gazing at him like he had handed her the keys to Fort Knox. "Thank you. Thank you so much for your kindness."

"You're welcome," he said gruffly, then turned to the desk clerk. "Is there somebody who can help with her bags?"

The clerk nodded and paged someone named Vernon to come to the front desk.

When he was certain the woman was taken care of, he walked back to the SUV. Now he only had to explain the situation to Kate.

And wonder how he would survive twelve hours of driving the next day on no sleep—except for one brief nap, tormented by dreams he had no business entertaining.

"I'm sorry again about this."

Kate, perched on the edge of one of the two double beds, gave Hunter an exasperated look. So they had to share a room. It wasn't the end of the world. He didn't have to glower like it was the worst thing that had ever happened to him. The man had spent more than two years in prison—as punishments went, sharing a hotel room with her shouldn't even rank in the same stratosphere.

"It's no big deal," she said again, trying not to be hurt by his obvious unease. "What else could you have done? That woman needed it worse than we did. I wouldn't have been able to sleep knowing we sent her on her way into that storm. You did exactly the right thing."

He didn't answer, just continued standing at the window gazing out at the snow still falling heavily.

Kate swallowed her sigh. What were they supposed to do

for the rest of the evening? It was far too early for bed and the idea of sitting in this hotel room with Hunter edgy and restless all evening was about as appealing as cleaning out an impacted bowel.

She stretched a little to take the driving kinks out of her back and was debating whether she should turn on the television set to watch the news when he turned from the window abruptly. "I'm going to take Belle for a walk."

"In the snow?"

"She needs the exercise. Anyway, I have a parka in the Jeep. I'll be fine. Do you want me to bring back something for dinner? On the way here, I saw a diner a block or so away that looked open."

"Sure. If they have some kind of soup and maybe a dinner salad, that would be great."

"What kind of soup do you like?"

"Any kind except broccoli."

"You're a physician. Don't you know broccoli is good for you?"

"Unfortunately, it's usually the things that aren't very good for me that I find the most desirable."

He made a sound that could have been a laugh. "You and me both, doc."

"Can you carry a take-out bag and hold Belle's leash at the same time?" she asked.

"I'm a man of many talents," he said dryly. "I'm sure I'll be fine."

Kate had to admit she was relieved when he slipped on Belle's leash and walked out of the hotel room. Her muscles seemed to relax and for the first time all day she felt as if she could take a deep breath into her lungs.

This was all so much harder than she thought it would be, spending every moment in close proximity. With each passing minute, she found something else attractive about him. By the time this trip was over, she was going to be a quivering mass of hormones.

Unless she did something about it. The thought whispered into her head, seductive and beguiling.

Maybe he wasn't completely immune to her. After he had awakened while she was driving, she thought she caught a glimpse of *something* in those midnight eyes, something dark and hot and hungry. He had quickly veiled it before she could be sure but there had been an instant there when she thought maybe that hunger had been directed at *her.*

The thought made her stomach muscles quiver. If she tried hard enough, perhaps she could seduce him. What better way to spend a snowy night trapped together in a hotel room than in each other's arms?

She rolled her eyes at herself. Right. As if she could entice a man like Hunter Bradshaw. She was just a master of seduction, wasn't she? That's why she was the only twenty-six-year-old virgin left in the civilized world.

To distract herself from such unproductive thoughts, she flipped on the television just in time to catch the end of the six-o'clock news. She watched the Albuquerque station for a few moments, long enough to learn the whole area was socked in by snow. When the news was over, she flipped through the twenty or so channels with little success.

Though she didn't necessarily feel like going out into the teeth of that storm, she could use some exercise to work out a little of this dangerous restlessness. The hotel didn't have a pool or an exercise room. About the only course open to her was walking the halls.

At least she could get some ice while she was up and moving, she decided. She found her room key and grabbed the ice bucket, then walked out into the hall just as the door to the room next door opened.

The woman in the doorway was lovely, with thick dark hair that brushed her shoulders and delicate light bronze features. She was also hugely pregnant, near the end of the third trimester, Kate thought.

This must be the woman Hunter had given their second room to. His career in the damsel-rescuing business was certainly off to a promising start.

She turned her sudden grin into a friendly smile and gestured to the ice bucket the woman held. Inside the room, she could see two dark-headed children propped on their stomachs on the bed watching cartoons.

"Hello. Looks like we're heading in the same direction. Can I fill that for you? That way you don't have to leave your children."

"That would be great." The woman mustered a strained smile that didn't conceal her sudden wince or the hand she placed on the small of her back.

Kate took the ice bucket from her and quickly filled them both, then returned to the room. The woman was still standing in her doorway, her expression pinched.

"Here you go," Kate said.

"Thank you."

"You're welcome. I'm Kate Spencer, by the way."

"Mariah Begay. You're with the nice man who gave us the room, aren't you?"

Nice? She didn't hear that word used in connection with Hunter Bradshaw very often. It should be, she thought. He *was* nice, even if he would probably jump down her throat if she ever called him that. What else would you call a man who had sacrificed at least a week of his life to help his sister's best friend?

She nodded. "Right."

"Thank you again for giving up your room. I hope it hasn't been too much of an inconvenience."

"Of course not." She smiled. "Your children are beautiful. I'm guessing they're about five and two, right?"

The woman's small smile revealed a narrow gap between her two front teeth. "Yes," she answered proudly. "Claudia will be six in February and Joey will be three next June."

"You're going to have your hands full with the little one."

"I know. But they're worth it." She winced again and pressed her hand to her back again. It was almost rhythmic, Kate thought, watching her carefully.

"I noticed you had Utah plates."

"Yes. My husband flies F-16s in the air force. He's stationed out of Hill Field but he's been in the Gulf for the last six months."

"Hunter and I are both from Salt Lake City."

Mariah's eyes widened. "I thought I recognized him! That's Hunter Bradshaw you're traveling with!"

Kate could feel her friendly smile cool and she braced herself to defend him. Hunter's case had been widely publicized in Utah. Dru Ferrin had been a popular television personality and her death had been front-page news for months, both in the aftermath of the murders and during the trial.

She doubted there was a resident of Utah who didn't know Hunter's name.

Even though his vindication and subsequent release had also been widely publicized, Kate knew there were many who still believed he got away with murder.

How he must hate his notoriety, she thought, aching for him.

"Yes," she said tersely.

"I followed the trial a little. I was bedridden during my

pregnancy with Joey so I had a lot of time to watch the news. I thought it was terrible what happened to him! A horrible injustice. Mike and I never thought he was guilty, even during the trial."

She pressed a hand to her back again and Kate wondered if she was even aware of it.

"You know it's not really safe for a woman past her eighth month to do a lot of traveling, especially not alone."

"I know." Grief spasmed across her face. "I wouldn't be here but my father died two days ago. Cancer. We knew it was coming."

"That doesn't make it any easier. I'm sorry."

"I had to come back to the Rez for the funeral. My mother doesn't have anyone else."

Kate watched her for a moment, wondering if she ought to mind her own business. But when Mariah pressed her hand to her back again, she couldn't contain her suspicions any longer.

"How long have you been having contractions?" she asked.

Mariah stared at her, her eyes as wide and dark as the desert at midnight. "I'm not!"

"You're having pain, though, aren't you?"

"Some. My back has been bothering me. But that's only because I've been driving for the last six hours."

"You would know, I suppose. Can I just point out that we've been standing here talking for ten minutes. I've counted the times you tense up and I'm up to four now. That's less than three minutes apart."

Mariah stared at her, her features slack. "You're…you're wrong. I can't be in labor! I'm only thirty-six weeks along!"

"Well, babies sometimes have their own timetables. One more week and your baby would be considered full-term."

"No," Mariah wailed. "I can't have my baby on the reservation! I can't! I swore when I left for college that any children I might have wouldn't be born here."

She seemed horrified at the very idea and Kate instinctively tried to calm her. "I'm sure there's fine medical care here. Shiprock is a good-sized town. They should have a clinic, at least."

"They do," Mariah said automatically. "They built a new one a few years ago. Farmington has a hospital too. That's where my father was treated during his illness. Maybe I should just try to make it there."

Before Kate could answer, Mariah moaned with pain and held both hands over her abdomen, as if Kate had made the contractions more real just by mentioning them.

"How far away is the Shiprock clinic?"

"I don't know. The other side of town. Three, maybe four miles."

"With these conditions, it will take at least ten or fifteen minutes to drive that." Kate frowned. "I'm not sure it's safe to try to make that, not as fast as these pains seem to be coming and not in this blizzard. Is there an ambulance service?"

Mariah looked taken aback by that and for the first time, she started to look scared.

"I…I think so. Do you really think that's necessary?"

"From what I've seen, your contractions are coming fast and regular. Without an internal exam I can't be certain, but I'm willing to bet you've been in labor all day without realizing it. You're probably close to fully dilated, which means that baby's going to be here soon, ready or not."

"Are you a nurse?"

Kate tried to look professional, something tough for somebody who wasn't even five feet four inches tall. "Doctor, actually. I'm in my second year of residency at the University of Utah."

Some of the fear seemed to ease in Mariah's eyes. "Oh thank heavens! Have you delivered any babies?"

"Three or four dozen."

Mariah grasped her hand. "Driving into that hotel parking lot was the best thing that's happened to me since Michael was sent to the Gulf."

"I believe I can deliver your baby if it comes to that but I'd really prefer to do it under better conditions than this, at least somewhere with a fetal monitor. I think we need to call an ambulance."

"Okay. Okay, whatever you think is best."

She bent over with another pain and Kate decided the time for discussion was over. She hurried to the phone.

"Don't leave me!"

"I'm not leaving. I'm just going to call the ambulance. Hang on, honey. Find a comfortable position and I'll be right back."

Mariah nodded and sank into the small armchair in the room, her eyes full of fear and pain and no small amount of trust.

Kate could only hope she would be worthy of it.

Chapter 6

The storm continued to howl and blow as Hunter made his slow, tedious way back to the hotel, the bag of takeout in one hand and Belle's leash in the other.

He had taken her as far and as long as he dared. At least she'd had plenty of exercise for the night. Walking into that ferocious wind made every step twice as much work.

By the time he'd circled the block twice and stopped at the diner down the street, his muscles burned as if he'd run a marathon.

The cook and solitary waitress had looked at him like he was crazy to venture out into the storm to the empty diner. He wasn't so sure they were wrong. Still, his stomach had rumbled pleasantly at the aromas of baking bread and fried onions.

Food was another thing that had held little interest to him since his release and he took heart at the idea that maybe that particular appetite was returning, too.

He ordered soup for Kate—a double order of chicken noodle with noodles that looked homemade—and beef Stroganoff for himself, and he had the waitress throw in two orders of boysenberry pie.

By the time the waitress packaged it up for him and sent him on his way with a warning to be careful, his earlier footprints had all but disappeared under the new onslaught of snow.

He made new ones as he trudged on, wishing his past could disappear as easily as those footprints in the snow. That he could be clean and new again.

At the hotel, warmth washed over him as he opened the door. With no free hands, he couldn't brush off the snow that coated his parka. He could only wish he could shake it all off like Belle did. Instead, it fell off in little clumps as he and Belle walked through the lobby and climbed the stairs to their second-floor room.

He let himself into the room, expecting to find Kate either asleep or curled up on one of those beds watching television. When he found the room empty, he frowned, concerned. Where could she be?

The hotel wasn't exactly overflowing with leisure diversions. No pool, no exercise room, not even an on-site restaurant. What else could have drawn her from the room?

He would have seen her on his way up if she'd gone down to the lobby for a little company. Where else could she be?

He took off his wet parka and hung it over the shower-curtain rod where it could drip into the tub, then put out food and water for Belle. While she chowed down, he ate a few bites of the beef Stroganoff while he tried to figure out where Kate might have disappeared to—and tried not to focus on the worry gnawing at his gut.

Was that her voice? He wondered at a low murmur from next door. It sounded like her along with the sound of children crying behind the door. Before he could analyze it further, he distinctly heard the sound of a woman crying out in pain.

Without taking a moment to think about it, he pulled his Glock out of his suitcase and rushed out into the hall, then banged on the door. "Kate? Kate, are you in there? Open up!"

He waited, his heart beating a loud cadence in his ears. When she opened the door, he darted his glance inside to assess the situation.

The two dark-haired children he had seen earlier were curled up together on one of the beds while the woman he'd given the room to was stretched out on the other one, her face drenched in sweat and her features contorted with pain.

He jerked his gaze back to Kate, who was looking at him with a naked relief that stunned him.

"Oh Hunter. I've never been so glad to see anybody in my life!"

Before he could respond, she dragged him into the room behind her. "Can you take Claudia and Joey over to our room and see if there's a movie on they might like? They're a little frightened right now."

"What's going on?" he asked in a harsh undertone, engaging the safety on his Glock and shoving it into the waistband of his jeans, at the small of his back, out of sight.

"We're having a baby. Well, Mariah's having a baby," she corrected. "I'm just helping."

"Now? Here?" His voice rose on the last word. The children, who had stopped crying momentarily, started up again and Kate's look of relief at seeing him shifted to one that bordered on dismay.

"We called an ambulance at least twenty minutes ago but Shiprock only has two crews and they're both out on traffic-accident calls right now. The dispatcher couldn't give us any idea how long it would take to get paramedics here."

Well, at least he wouldn't have to worry about spending the evening staring at the walls of the hotel room to keep from jumping Kate. Thank the Lord for small favors.

"What do you need me to do?"

The woman on the bed moaned again. "I'm coming, Mariah," Kate said in a calm, reassuring voice at odds with the slight panic in her eyes. "I'll be right there. Hang on."

She quickly turned back to Hunter but he could tell her attention was on her patient. "If you can keep the children entertained in our room, that would be a huge help. Maybe they'd like to play with Belle."

What did he know about a couple of kids? He shifted his gaze to the two rug rats watching him with tearstained dark eyes. He hated to admit it but he'd rather be helping deliver the baby than be in charge of a couple of bawling kids. And he wanted to deliver a baby about as badly as he wanted to strip naked and run through the streets of Shiprock in the middle of that blizzard.

But Kate was looking at him with such faith and entreaty in her expression he knew he didn't have a choice. He tried not to let her see how daunted he was by his assignment. "Okay. Sure. No problem."

Famous last words. It took every ounce of guile he possessed to convince the children to come through the connecting door. They didn't want to let their mother out of their sight, so he agreed to leave the door open and at last they came with cautious curiosity once he let Belle out of her kennel.

To his great relief, the dog worked her usual magic. The

children were nervous at first around her but as soon as they realized Belle was a big softy, they relaxed. In a few moments, the three of them were happily wrestling on the floor.

There. That wasn't so tough. With a thoroughly ridiculous sense of accomplishment, Hunter helped the girl find Belle's favorite rubber bone from her pile of supplies and showed her how to toss it to the other side of the room.

Each time Belle padded after it with a weary, puzzled obedience, the two children giggled as if she were wearing clown shoes and a big rubber nose.

As they seemed to be sufficiently distracted, Hunter returned to the connecting doors between the rooms so he could watch the drama unfolding next door.

Kate Spencer in action was an incredible sight, one he couldn't manage to wrench his eyes from.

She never seemed to stop moving—she wiped the forehead and held the hand of the distressed mother; she called the hotel desk clerk for extra linens; she measured and timed contractions; she took heartbeats and blood pressures and temperatures; all the while she kept watch out the window through the whirling snow for the paramedics with an expression on her face that seemed to grow more worried by the moment.

A cell phone buzzed suddenly on the bedside table and the woman—Mariah, Kate had called her—grabbed for it.

"Oh Michael," Mariah said, then began to weep. The baby's father? Hunter assumed so, by her reaction.

He wasn't trying to eavesdrop but he couldn't help hearing snippets of her side of the conversation. "I should never have tried to come by myself. I know. I'm so sorry. I wish you could be here. I miss you so much."

Kate wandered over to him during the phone call to give Mariah a little more privacy. "Her husband is a pilot out of

Hill Air Force Base," she told him. "He's stationed in the Persian Gulf. Her father died of cancer a few days ago and she's come home to the reservation to help her mother with arrangements."

"That's tough." He was suddenly vastly relieved he had gone with his instincts and surrendered this room to the woman.

"How's it going in there?" she asked.

He glanced back at the children, who had finally tired of catch and were snuggling on the floor with Belle while they watched the animated movie he'd found on cable. The girl looked like she was going to nod off any minute while the younger boy seemed hypnotized by the movie.

"Fine. What about you?"

She aimed a careful look toward Mariah Begay. When she saw the woman was still wrapped up in her phone conversation with her husband, Kate turned back to him with a frown. "Not as well as I'd hoped. The baby is a frank breech. If we were in a hospital I would recommend a C-section to get him out quickly but I don't think we're going to make it in time. He's already moved down into the birth canal."

"What can you do?"

"Try to help Mariah hang on until the paramedics get here. With any luck, that will be soon."

"She's in better hands with you than with some frazzled paramedics." The gruff words sounded awkward and stilted but he meant every word.

Her eyes widened at the compliment and she gazed at him with such touched gratitude that he had to grip his hands into fists to keep from reaching for her right there, despite the circumstances.

Before he could do something so foolish, Mariah moaned a little and Kate hurried back to her patient's side.

* * *

Twenty minutes later, Kate's nerves were as tightly wound as a bowstring and she was as sweat-soaked as Mariah.

She had never felt so inept, all fumbling hands and indecision. During her ob-gyn rotation, she had participated in dozens of deliveries but only a handful of *those* had presented in labor as breech. All but two of those had resulted in C-sections.

Her total sum of experience was in the controlled environment of a sterile, well-equipped hospital with all the latest diagnostic equipment, not in a small, slightly shabby motel in Shiprock, New Mexico, where she had little but a stethoscope.

Every decision she made here seemed life or death. Never had she felt the pressure of her oath more keenly.

If only those blasted paramedics would get here!

She turned back to her patient. "Okay, I need you to hold on, Mariah. Breathe, sweetheart. Try not to push."

"I have to push," the woman wailed. "I can't stop!"

Kate drew in a ragged breath. She was afraid they were past the point of no return here. The baby was coming, ready or not.

She would just have to make sure they *were* ready. A quick check told her the baby's rump was already presenting.

Every moment she continued to try to delay delivery increased the chance of cord prolapse, where the blood and oxygen supplies were cut off from the baby with each uterine contraction.

Fear was a heavy weight in her stomach, but she recognized she had no choice.

While she was considering the best course of action, she

caught sight of Hunter. He had angled his chair in the connecting doorway so he had a view into both rooms. Kate couldn't see Claudia, but Hunter held little Joey on his lap and the boy was sound asleep.

The sight of Hunter looking so solid and big, his eyes a deep, concerned blue, gave her an odd sense of comfort. She felt a little less alone.

She turned back to Mariah. "Okay, let's do this."

The hotel staff had supplied them with every clean towel in the place. They had already stripped the bed of all its linens and covered it with a plastic sheet, also supplied by the nervous desk clerk. Now Kate spread several layers of towels under Mariah and had her scoot to the edge of the bed.

"I want you to lie on your side. It's going to be a little awkward to deliver that way but that position will increase blood flow to the baby. That's important right now since we don't have any real way of checking for fetal distress."

"I don't care how hard it is. Just keep my son safe!"

Kate settled her into position just as another contraction hit her. Mariah cried out. "I have to push."

"Okay. Go for it."

With Kate offering encouragement and positioning help, it only took two pushes for the baby's legs and torso to slide free.

"You'll be happy to know your OB was right. It's still a boy. One more push and you'll be able to hold him. Come on, now."

This was the trickiest part. A dozen possible complications rattled through her mind as she supported the baby's torso in the crook of one arm and inserted the fingers of her other hand inside the uterus to keep the cervix from contracting around the baby's neck and strangling him.

On one high, thin cry, Mariah pushed again and pushed out the baby's head in a gush of blood and fluid.

"Lots of hair on this one," Kate said, trying to hide her fear at the baby's blue color. "He's a tiny one."

Mariah started to weep and shake in reaction. "Why isn't he crying? What's wrong? Is he okay?"

Out of the corner of her eye, she saw Hunter rise to his feet, the boy still sleeping in his arms, but she had no more than half a second to register that. "I'm working on him. Let me clean him up."

With the bulb syringe from her medical kit, she suctioned out the tiny boy's nasal passages, then rubbed him vigorously with a clean towel, both to clean off the birth fluids and to wake up his nervous system.

The baby wasn't breathing on his own, though his little heart was still beating. She had to hope he was getting some oxygen from the placenta that Mariah had yet to deliver but without a monitor, it was impossible to know for sure.

She needed to get him breathing fast. Off the table she'd set up as an improvised instrument tray for the few inadequate supplies she had with her, Kate grabbed her pocket mask and covered the infant's nose and mouth.

She gave two gentle puffs of air and saw the infant's lungs expand. *Come on kiddo,* she thought. *Take over now.*

Her own heart raced as she waited. Just when she was afraid she would have to start compressions, the infant gurgled a little then started to cry, weak at first then building in intensity.

Kate grinned as a vast relief washed over her. "There you go. You get good and mad at me. That's the way," she crooned, wiping off the rest of the fluids then wrapping the tiny figure in another towel before handing him to Mariah.

"Will he be all right?"

"He's pinking up great now. He's tiny, probably no more than five pounds, but I think he'll be just fine."

For a few moments, Kate admired the elementally beautiful sight of a mother holding the tiny life she had brought into the world, then she got down to business cutting the cord and delivering the placenta.

Just as she was wrapping things up, voices and a flurry of activity in the hallway signaled the arrival of the paramedics—a good hour after they'd been called.

"I guess this is our patient?" A burly Navajo with a solid chest and two thick braids led the way with a stretcher.

"Yeah, but now you get two for the price of one," Kate answered.

"Bonus." He grinned at her and then at the new mother and her baby. His eyes widened when he saw the woman. "Mariah Begay? That you?"

"Charlie Yazzi! Last I heard you were in Phoenix." Mariah's eyes lit up despite her obvious exhaustion.

"No. I married a woman of the Bitter Water clan, born for the Salt Clan. My wife, her folks live here. She wanted to be close to them so we been back in Shiprock for a few years now." His features sobered. "Heard about your pop. I guess you came back to the Rez for his funeral, yeah?"

Mariah nodded and held her baby just a little tighter.

"Mike with you?" the paramedic asked.

She shook her head, her chin wobbling a little, but didn't speak as the other paramedic started checking vitals.

"He's stationed in Iraq and is trying to swing leave right now," Kate said quietly.

"You're by yourself? Didn't I hear you already had two little kids?"

Mariah gestured to the other room, then sudden panic flickered across her tired features. "Joey and Claudia! I can't leave them here. What will I do with them while I'm at the hospital until my mom can come up from Naschitti?"

Kate started to offer to watch them but Charlie Yazzi cut her off. "They can stay at our place tonight. Marilyn and the kids will love the company. My house is just a block away and she can be here in five minutes to get them. Don't even think about arguing. It's the least we can do. Now let's get you two to the hospital, where you belong."

Forty-five minutes later, Kate shut the door after Charlie Yazzi's wife had bundled up Claudia and Joey and taken them out into the night.

The room seemed unnaturally quiet after all the chaos of the evening.   She turned back to find Hunter standing in the connecting doorway, his midnight eyes glittering.

"Wow. You sure know how to show a guy a good time."

She laughed even as exhaustion seeped through her, so overwhelming she suddenly felt as if her bones had dissolved.

He moved toward her. "Seriously, you were incredible, Kate. Watching you in there was the most amazing thing I've ever seen in my life. That baby would have died if you hadn't been here, wouldn't it?"

She shrugged. "I don't know if I'd go that far."

"I would. I saw how blue he was and how worried you were. Then you were working on him and suddenly he was this crying little creature, flailing his arms around and looking normal."

"No matter how many babies I deliver, it still hits me hard every time. Knowing I'm the very first one to welcome this new little person to the world is an indescribable feeling."

"Wasn't it Carl Sandburg who said a baby is God's opinion that the world should go on?"

Her insides quivered at hearing such a tender sentiment from a man who had been forced to walk a hard, ugly road.

She thought of the child he had thought was his, the tiny boy who had been murdered with Dru Ferrin, and grieved for him.

She gave him a watery smile. "I'll have to remember that one."

"You never ate your soup," he said. "I could probably find a microwave somewhere in the hotel and heat it for you."

She tried to assess her appetite and decided exhaustion trumped her hunger. "Thanks anyway, but I just want to sleep."

She looked at the room where she had delivered the baby. The desk clerk had sent housekeeping in as soon as the paramedics had left for the hospital and there was no trace now of the miraculous event.

"I guess since Mariah and her kids won't be using this room, we don't need to double up after all. I'll just use this one."

Some unfathomable expression flickered in his eyes, something she feared might be relief, but he quickly veiled his expression. "Right."

"I'll just grab my things then and move them over here."

"I'll get it. Sit down for a moment."

She ignored his order. If she sat down, she would probably fall instantly asleep.

Fatigue was a heavy weight around her shoulders. Little wonder at it, she thought. They had survived a tumultuous day, emotionally as well as physically. Nine hours on the road, a blizzard, and a frank-breech delivery. She had to hope the rest of their trip would proceed a little more smoothly or they might never make it to Florida.

He returned a moment later with her suitcase. "Here you go." He set it on the folding chrome luggage rack in the small closet, then turned to go back to the adjoining room.

She roused herself enough to stop him with a hand on
his arm.

"Thank you, Hunter. Not just for the suitcase. For everything. I was scared tonight." She could admit it now. "I've
never had to deliver a baby under these kind of conditions
and it was a complicated delivery. I was doubting every decision I made. But then I looked at you and you were watching me with complete faith. I can't tell you how much that
meant to me."

His eyes darkened suddenly, the black of his pupil nearly
consuming the blue as he met her gaze. "You're welcome,"
he said gruffly.

The atmosphere between them seemed to pop and sizzle
and she couldn't look away from the intensity of those glittering eyes. Against her will, her gaze shifted downward
slightly and she found herself staring at his hard, unsmiling
mouth.

She was still holding his arm, she realized. His skin was
hot beneath her fingers and the muscle of his biceps was
tight, hard as granite.

She swallowed, trying to summon the will to release his
arm. Just as she started to move her fingers, her gaze met
his again and she froze at the raw heat in his eyes.

She thought she made some kind of sound but it was
swallowed when his mouth captured hers.

In an instant her exhaustion trickled away, leaving only
a stunned and fiery heat. So long. She had wanted him to kiss
her for so very long. To find herself in his arms seemed an
impossible dream, something she had hardly dared hope for.

She had an odd, random memory of being six years old,
moving from town to town with Brenda, never knowing
where their next meal would come from. On the TV of some
dingy motel room or other she had seen a commercial for a

Cabbage Patch Kids doll and she had wanted one with every fiber of her little six-year-old heart.

Of course, she had known better than even to ask Brenda, but that hadn't stopped her from hoping and praying.

That year at Christmastime Brenda had found herself between men—and jobs—so they had wound up living in a Miami homeless shelter. Some do-good organization had brought toys for all the children. Kate could still remember her instant of heart-stopping, stunned glee when she had opened her present to find exactly the kind of doll she'd dreamed of, the kind she'd never thought she would have.

Kissing Hunter Bradshaw was a million times better than getting the toy of her dreams.

He was big and solid and wonderful and she kissed him back with all the eager enthusiasm she had never been able to give another man.

Every single nerve cell in her body hummed with need and she wanted to wrap her arms around those hard muscles and hang on for the rest of her life.

His hunger was a slumbering beast that suddenly roared awake, wild and barbaric and urgently ravenous.

Mindless, heedless, he devoured Kate's mouth with his tongue and his teeth, tasting and biting and sucking.

She tasted like vanilla sugar, like everything sweet he had ever craved. She was small and curvy and he wanted to wrap himself around her, inside her.

He gripped her soft hair with one hand to angle her mouth for his kiss and slid his other to the seat of her jeans, drawing her closer to his instant, fierce arousal.

Heaven.

This was better than any half-baked fantasy of making love on some sandy beach. This was real. *She* was real.

He wasn't sure how long they stood in that connecting doorway, mouths and bodies tangled together. He lost track of time, of everything, until she made a soft sound low in her throat and he realized she was trembling.

What the hell was he doing?

A tiny, insidious voice of reason slithered through his ravenous hunger. He wrenched his mouth away, his heartbeat thundering in his ears.

Another few seconds and he would have ripped off her clothes and impaled her against the wall.

She was exhausted, so tired she could barely stand up, and he was taking advantage of that to ease his own lust. His hands fell away and he forced himself to step back a pace even as his body howled at the loss of physical contact he hadn't even realized he had been so desperately craving.

Kate looked tousled and windblown, as if she'd just come from the blizzard outside. His fingers had played havoc with her hair, her cheeks were flushed, and her mouth was swollen from his kiss.

Finally he met her gaze and found her staring at him with an odd, unreadable expression in her blue eyes. He was afraid to look too closely, not sure he could bear seeing the same disgust there that he suddenly felt for himself.

Before his arrest, he had always considered himself immune to the world's opinion of him. He had become a cop when his father and the rest of those in the Judge's social circle had tried to discourage him, when some had openly disdained him for his career choice.

His father had pushed him and Taylor both hard to go into law. Hunter might have considered it if not for the constant pressure—which, predictably, made him contrary enough to run in the opposite direction.

When he had applied and been accepted to the police

academy, the Judge had been furious at his stubbornness. Friends had called him crazy but Hunter hadn't cared.

He had always prided himself in going his own way, impervious to what others thought of him.

After his arrest, it had been a bitter lesson to discover he *did* care what the world thought of him. He cared deeply. He had hated knowing people deemed him the kind of monster capable of killing two women, of taking the life of an unborn baby.

He suddenly discovered that this woman's opinion of him mattered far more than the rest of the world.

He didn't want her to think he was some kind of monster, some kind of rampaging beast. But he had certainly behaved like one.

She continued staring at him, her eyes huge and solemn, and he knew he had to say something.

"Kate, I—" *I'm sorry* would have been a lie he couldn't quite bring himself to utter and any other words seemed to lodge in his throat.

After a long moment, she let out a breath. "We have a long day tomorrow." Her fingers curled around the doorknob between their rooms. "We'd both better get some rest."

He could think of a million things to say but he couldn't seem to work any of them past the lump of self-disgust in his throat.

"Right. You're right," he finally said. "Good night, then."

She all but pushed him through the door and closed it with a decisive click behind him.

He closed his own connecting door, then stood on the other side for a long time, hungry and aching and ashamed of the beast he had let prison turn him into.

Chapter 7

"He's beautiful, Mariah. Absolutely gorgeous."

Kate smiled down at the little blanket-wrapped bundle in her arms. Big dark eyes studied her solemnly from underneath a tiny blue knit cap. The boy had dusky, delicate features and a little cupid bow of a mouth. He smelled wonderful, of baby lotion and milk and brand-new life, an irresistible smell that made her want to sink her face into his softness and just inhale for a few hours.

He yawned suddenly and flailed one curled fist out of the bunting toward his mouth like a little kitten ready to lick a paw and Kate tumbled completely into love, as she had with every single infant she'd ever helped deliver.

She had toyed with obstetrics as her specialty because she loved moments like this so much, knowing she had a small but important part in helping these little ones arrive safely.

In the end she decided she liked the idea of family medicine more, the variety of treating a grandmother's arthritis one moment and a five-year-old with tonsillitis the next, of being the first line of defense in the fight to keep her patients healthy.

Holding this little one was definitely enough to make her reconsider, though.

Propped in the hospital bed and looking radiantly maternal, Mariah smiled. "He has Michael's eyes and my nose. Not a bad combination."

"Have you heard from your husband today?"

"Yes!" Mariah beamed. "He's coming home! He called me this morning, right after he was granted leave for two weeks. He probably won't make it for my father's funeral tomorrow but he'll be here by the end of the week. He's hoping he can swing being transferred back to the States in the next month or so."

"I'm so happy for you." Kate smiled, stroking the soft skin of the baby's cheek. She laughed when he rooted toward her finger. "What name did you decide on?"

"Franklin James Begay, after my father. We'll call him Jamie. It seemed right."

"It's a good strong name for a healthy little baby."

"He wouldn't be here if not for you. I don't know how to thank you for what you did."

Mariah's gaze landed on Hunter standing silently in the doorway and her smile widened to include him. "Both of you. I hate even thinking about what I would have done if I had been alone. If you hadn't given up one of your rooms for us, I could have gone into labor on the road somewhere in the middle of the blizzard with only the children to help me. Jamie wouldn't be here if it weren't for you."

"I'm glad things worked out the way they did," Hunter said quietly.

Kate risked a look under her lashes at him. Instead of looking at Mariah, he was watching her hold the baby, his expression unreadable again.

She would give anything to know what thoughts were spinning around in that head of his. Probably reconsidering this whole damsel in distress rescue thing. Wishing he were back in his mountain hideaway, away from emergency deliveries and fretting infants and twenty-six-year-old virgins with mortifying crushes.

To keep from blushing and embarrassing herself further, she held the baby out to him. "Here. You were part of this whole thing, Hunter. You should hold him."

Alarm flickered in the stormy dark blue of his eyes. "No, really. That's okay."

"Come on."

She didn't give him much of a choice, just transferred the tiny bundle into his arms. For a moment Hunter held tiny baby with awkward reluctance, like a ball player about to bobble a catch.

After just a moment, he tightened his hold. His hands looked huge around that tiny bundle, square-tipped and strong, and the sight plucked funny little strings inside her

He relaxed by degrees, until finally the nervousness gave way to a baffled kind of wonder.

Franklin James Begay tolerated the manhandling for a few precious moments and Kate cherished up the image of big, tough ex-cop and ex-con Hunter Bradshaw staring into tiny, solemn eyes. Soon hunger won out, though, and the baby let out a couple of squawks and started flailing those little fists around.

One side of Hunter's mouth lifted and he handed him back to his mother with alacrity. "He's got good lungs anyway."

Mariah smiled. "I have a feeling things won't be quiet at our house, with three kids demanding my attention every moment."

"You, ah, had better feed him," Hunter said. "Kate, we should probably go soon. We've got a long drive."

"Right." Kate rose obediently, though she didn't want this visit to end—not necessarily because she loved holding new life, though she did, but more because she dreaded climbing into that SUV again and enduring hours of tension.

All morning, the ghost of the kiss they shared the night before seemed to seethe and stir around them as they checked out of their hotel and shared a quick breakfast at the cafe down the street, the same place where Hunter had picked up her uneaten dinner.

She saw his muscles flex as he loaded her suitcase into the Jeep and remembered the hard strength of those arms around her. She watched him take a bite of his ham and cheese omelette and remembered how those teeth had nipped at her lip.

She tried to be surreptitious about it but she couldn't seem to help noticing little details like that about him while Hunter would barely even *look* at her all morning. When he did, his eyes were always remote, veiled, and she felt as if she were talking to the mast-shaped mountain that gave Shiprock its name.

She wasn't sure she could endure two or three more days of this before they reached Miami.

What was the big deal anyway? They were two adults, both unattached. If they wanted to share a passionate, toe-curling kiss at the end of a crazy, stressful day, it certainly wasn't the end of the world.

He seemed to think it was, though. Though the kiss followed them around like a ghost, neither of them mentioned it until they left Shiprock heading across the eastern border of the reservation toward Farmington and the hospital.

"It won't happen again," Hunter suddenly said out of the blue after they had been on the road for ten minutes or so.

Though she knew exactly what he was talking about, she pretended ignorance. "What won't?"

His face looked carved from granite, harsh and austere. "I don't make a habit of accosting women in hotel rooms. I don't want you to be on your guard all the time around me, afraid I'm going to suddenly grab you."

Maybe I want *you to grab me,* she thought, but couldn't quite find the courage to say the words.

Hunter had stared out the windshield, his jaw tight and his mouth firm. "It was a momentary lapse in judgment, one I swear to you won't happen again. That said, I understand if you're uncomfortable now. I can arrange a flight home for you when we reach Albuquerque."

She didn't want to admit how tempting she found his suggestion. Now that she had something concrete to focus on instead of just vague awareness—like how fragile and feminine she had felt in his arms and how he kissed her like his life depended on it—this trip was bound to be hell.

Still, she couldn't give up. She wouldn't, if only to prove to herself that she was made of stronger stuff.

"Don't be ridiculous," she had snapped. "I'm going with you to find Brenda. Did you really think a little thing like a kiss between friends would send me running home?"

His only answer had been to draw those lips even tighter and turn his attention back to the road.

Oh, she couldn't *wait* to get back into that SUV for more of the same. Kate pushed away the depression settling on her shoulders and smiled at Mariah now. "Hunter is right. We should be on our way. But we have to keep in touch."

From her purse, she pulled out a business card. On the back she had added all her contact information—her home phone, cell, snail mail and e-mail addresses.

She handed the card to Mariah. "I'm going to want pictures of little Franklin James. He was my first—and hopefully only—hotel birth and I want to keep tabs on him."

"I'll contact you after I get back to Utah," Mariah promised.

"Good."

Kate hugged her, baby and all, and received more effusive thanks and even a few tears. To her secret delight, when Kate stood up, Mariah held her arms out to embrace Hunter too. Hunter complied a little stiffly but Mariah didn't seem to notice.

They said their goodbyes and a few moments later they walked out of the hospital into the thin December sunshine.

The storm's fury had blown itself out in the early-morning hours and Kate had awakened in the strange hotel room to the sound of snow plows and life returning to normal. Already, the sunshine had started to melt the thin layer remaining on the road and storm seemed as much a memory as that kiss.

He held the door open for her, as she had come to realize was an ingrained habit. She slid inside, trying hard to ignore the tremble of her insides at the scent of soap and expensive aftershave that clung to him.

Belle barked a quick greeting then settled back in her crate as Hunter climbed in then drove out of the parking lot and headed southeast, toward Albuquerque and the interstate.

"You looked good holding little Franklin," she said once they left Farmington behind and headed across the raw, stark beauty of the snow-covered high desert. "A bit more practice and you'll be a natural, just in time for any little ones Wyatt and Taylor might have. Or one of your own, I guess."

If she hadn't been watching, she might have missed the tiny flex of a muscle in his jaw. Was that grief in his eyes?

Suddenly she again remembered the child that had died along with Dru Ferrin, the child Hunter had believed was his.

"I'm sorry, Hunter." She wished she could slide right into the upholstery and disappear. "I wasn't thinking at all. I made you hold that baby, completely forgetting that it was probably painful for you after the child you lost."

His fingers stiffened around the steering wheel. "Most people would say I didn't really lose anything. The baby wasn't born yet and he wasn't even mine."

"I would never say that. I know what you lost."

He looked surprised by her words. "This is horrible to say but I think I grieved more for that baby than I did for Dru, even after I found out I wasn't his father. DNA tests weren't important to me. He was my son, in every way that mattered."

"Of course he was." Kate curled her hands in her lap from reaching out to him in comfort at his blunt confession. Given the tension between them, she didn't think he would welcome her touch right now.

She wondered if he was remembering, as she was, those months before the murders. To his sister's surprise, Hunter had been ecstatic about the baby. He had read baby books and gone ecstatic with Dru to Lamaze class and showed off ultrasound pictures to anyone within reach. She could still remember trying to smile woodenly and look excited for him.

She knew he had begged Dru to marry him when she told him she was pregnant and that she had continued to refuse, right up to her murder.

Kate had watched Hunter become more thrilled about the birth of the child—and increasingly frustrated with Dru's refusal to marry him—and she had wanted to grab the woman and shake her until her teeth rattled out for the careless, callous way she treated him.

"You would have been a wonderful father," she murmured.

"Maybe then. Not anymore." As soon as he said the words, he looked as if he regretted them.

"Why not?"

He gazed out at the desert. "I'm a different man than I was then. Harder. Less forgiving. Doing time on Death Row has a way of taking away all the good and leaving a man with nothing. I'm not a good bet for a father anymore. Or anything else."

His last words were pitched so low she had to strain to hear them over the humming of the tires on asphalt. Was that some kind of warning? she wondered.

If so, she was afraid it was coming far too late to do her any good.

Without the weather to slow them down, they made good time once they passed through Albuquerque. Traffic was relatively light and they didn't hit any delays.

All night as he had stared at the textured ceiling of the motel room berating himself for losing his head and giving into the heat, Hunter worried things between them would be tense and uncomfortable for the rest of this journey.

It wasn't as bad as he'd feared. Though he couldn't stop remembering their kiss and the hot and urgent hunger that still gnawed at him, with every mile he drove more of the thick tension seemed to seep away.

He wasn't sure he would ever feel completely comfortable around her, not with this constant attraction simmering beneath his skin. But he could at least try to be polite.

Prison might have distilled his psyche down to the bare elements of raw survival but he wasn't a wild animal in a cage anymore. It was time he started acting like a civilized human being again.

Between Albuquerque and Amarillo, she seemed content to listen to the radio—country music stations, mostly—and read her brother's book. They made only one stop to gas up and exercise Belle.

She offered to drive again when they finished their pit stop but he was wary about relinquishing the wheel. The last time she drove, he had spent the time in the middle of a hot, erotic dream that had most likely contributed to his boorish behavior later in the evening.

When they were back on the highway, Kate picked up her book again but she seemed restless. He was aware of every move and knew when her attention wandered. Though the book was still open on her lap, she spent more time looking out the window, her expression pensive.

What forces had shaped her into the woman she had become? He wondered. Strong and gutsy, brave enough to delivery a baby under relatively primitive conditions yet nervous about confronting her painful past.

He wanted to know about her, he realized. The information would be helpful for finding the woman she had always believed to be her mother. It might also help him understand the woman Kate had become.

"How old were you when this Brenda Golightly turned you over to the system?"

She looked as startled by his question as if he'd suddenly pulled over and started eating road kill. "Where did that come from?"

"Just wondering. Trying to figure everything out. I like to have all the pieces of the puzzle in front of me so I can see how they fit. I guess it's the detective in me."

He thought for a moment she wasn't going to answer him. She took a deep, steadying breath, the fingers of her left hand clenched on the armrest. He couldn't see her eyes behind her sunglasses but he thought he could guess at the emotions in them. Remembering her past obviously wasn't a gleeful skip down memory lane.

"Seven. I was seven years old."

"You spent four years with her then, after you were kidnapped from the McKinnons' front yard."

"Right." Her voice was terse.

"Why then, do you think? Why keep you only four years?"

"It wasn't like she made some kind of conscious choice in the matter. She went on a three-day bender and left me alone in a motel room with no food or running water. After two days when I couldn't bear the hunger pains anymore, I finally ventured out looking for something to eat. A cop found me rooting through a garbage can outside a doughnut shop."

Hunter's own stomach twisted at the cool, almost clinical way she described what must have been a terrifying childhood, full of hunger and fear and uncertainty.

"It was a stupid mistake," she went on in that same eerily calm voice. "I knew better than to go anywhere near a cop hangout. Brenda taught me early to avoid cops and social workers and anybody else who might ask too many questions. When I grew old enough to figure out that wasn't normal behavior, I just thought it was just because of our transient lifestyle. But knowing what I do now, I can't help thinking there was likely a more sinister explanation. She was probably afraid of someone finding out about Charlotte McKinnon being kidnapped and somehow link the two of us together."

She spoke about her true identity as if Charlotte McKinnon was a completely different person. He supposed in a way, she was.

"What happened after you were removed from her custody?"

She shrugged and adjusted her sunglasses higher on her nose. "Foster care. I moved around a lot at first. Nine placements in five years."

His own childhood hadn't exactly been easy, but he couldn't imagine what it would have been like never knowing stability. Even when his mother was at her worst shortly before her death, he always knew he had a home. The same four walls, the same bedroom furniture, the same grandfather clock ticking away in the hallway.

The Judge had been a harsh, autocratic father in many ways, but Hunter had never doubted his father loved him, even if that love had been more controlling than kind most of the time.

He couldn't imagine being seven years old, living with strangers, shuffled from place to place.

"Why so many?"

"My fault, mostly. I was confused, angry. Unmanageable. I guess you could say I didn't play well with others."

"Why not?"

"What did I know about other kids? Brenda always kept me away from anybody close to my own age. I didn't have any friends and of course I never went to school."

"At all?"

She shook her head. "Teachers and principals tend to ask nosy questions. We were never in one place long enough for school officials to come after us and drag me to class. So there I was a seven-year-old kindergartner. Luckily I'd taught myself to read—cereal boxes, mostly. The Kellogg Corporation was responsible for most of my nutrition during those years. Thank the Lord for fortified cereal."

"You must have caught up, education-wise. You're only, what, twenty-six, and you've already finished med school."

"I skipped a couple grades later and finished my undergrad work in three years. Those first few years after I was removed from Brenda's custody were tough, though. I had no idea how to interact socially with others. I lied, I stole from my foster parents, I beat up other kids at school and at home. And that was on my good days."

He couldn't quite swallow the idea of delicate, lovely Kate Spencer battling it out on the schoolground.

"Hey, don't laugh," she said at the amused look he sent her. "I was a tough little scrapper. I made up for what I didn't have in size in sheer evil ingenuity. One time I was mad at a foster mom for making me pitch in and help with laundry so I gleefully emptied a whole gallon of bleach on four baskets of clean clothes. That little tantrum of mine ruined just about every stitch of clothing in the house. Not a pretty sight. I was out of there by dinnertime."

"You were in pain and children in pain lash out."

"Oh, I lashed out with a vengeance." Her features softened. "Finally when I was twelve I got lucky. I was placed with Tom and Maryanne Spencer. They were an older couple who never had any children of their own. I was the third foster child they had taken in. The other two were both in college when they accepted me."

"They were good to you?"

Her smile was soft, tender, and gave her such an air of fragile beauty that Hunter had to remind himself to keep his eyes on the road. What he really wanted to do was bask in the glow of that smile, even if it wasn't directed at him.

"Wonderful. Maryanne is the most gentle, patient woman I've ever known. No matter how hard I scratched and clawed and fought to keep them away, she always returned my anger with love. And Tom's a doctor. Family medicine."

"That where you got the bug?"

"Yeah. I guess so. Whenever I had a day off from school, he would take me to his practice with him to file paperwork or stock supplies. The summer before my senior year in high school he took me on a three-week medical mission to central America. It was an incredible experience to watch this humble, unassuming man change people's lives. I watched the rapport he had with his patients, both in Central America and in his regular practice, and knew I wanted to be just like him someday."

"Looks like you're on your way."

She shook her head. "I have a long journey ahead of me if I want to follow in the footsteps of Tom Spencer."

"They must be proud of you. Taylor told me you went on your own medical trip to Guatemala last month."

"Whatever I've become, I owe to them. I don't know where I would have ended up if not for them. Probably just like Brenda—an addict on the streets. They saved me."

She didn't give herself nearly enough credit, he thought. All the best intentions in the world mean nothing if they don't find receptive ground to take root.

Despite the insecurity and trauma of those years with Brenda Golightly and her first few years in foster care, Kate had become a remarkable woman. He wanted to say so but the words clogged in his throat.

"You still keep in touch with the Spencers?" he asked instead.

"Oh, yes. We e-mail all the time and I go back to St. Petersburg as often as possible. I spent Thanksgiving with them a year ago but I haven't been able to schedule another visit in a while."

"Maybe if we have time, we could stop on the way back through."

She lowered her sunglasses for just a moment but the delight in her eyes sent warmth trickling through him.

"That would be great!"

He was in trouble, Hunter thought as they once more lapsed into silence. Deep, deep trouble. Every moment he spent with her not only added fuel to the fire of his growing desire for her but made him think all kinds of tender thoughts he had no business entertaining.

She had been through enough in her life. She didn't need the added complication of a bitter ex-con who had no idea where he fit into the world anymore.

To her relief, her few answers about her history seemed to satisfy Hunter's sudden curiosity. He turned his attention back to the road and the easy, rolling hills of West Texas. After a while she pulled out her brother's book again.

She was having a harder time focusing today. Despite Wyatt's intricately crafted story, the words seemed to blur on the page and she couldn't seem to concentrate. Images from the past seemed to crowd everything else out and she once more felt like that skinny, frightened seven-year-old with an empty stomach and a two-day-old bear claw in her hand, facing down that bald, fatherly looking cop.

What she had told him was ugly enough but she wondered what Hunter would say if he knew she had whitewashed some of it.

She hated thinking about that time in her life before she went to live with the Spencers.

Kate was sure all the well-meaning social workers thought they were rescuing her from a horrible fate when they took her from Brenda Golightly. She had no doubt they were, but some of the situations she had been thrust into during those first five years in foster care had only been slightly less terrible.

Ugly things could happen to a young girl with few social defenses, things that made her feel sick inside to remember.

In her first foster home, a fourteen-year-old sexual predator-in-training had seen a frightened little girl as a convenient victim.

The first few times he touched her, she had been too stunned and sickened and too afraid to do anything to defend herself. The next time he came to her room, she had been ready for him with a kitchen knife she had carefully hidden in the folds of her nightgown when she went into the kitchen for one last glass of water before bed.

When the little bastard tried his funny stuff again, she had pulled the knife out from beneath her pillow and stabbed him in the leg. She hadn't been strong enough to shove the blade in very deep but he had screamed and cried and bled all over her room until his parents came running to the rescue.

Nobody believed her version of events, of course. Why should they? She was just the white-trash troublemaking kid of a junkie who attacked an innocent boy without provocation.

After that, she was labeled a Problem Child. And she had done her best to live up to that reputation. She became suspicious, wild, angry, rejecting anybody who tried to reach out to her.

The Spencers had been her final chance, the last-ditch whistlestop before she was shipped to juvenile detention. She fought their efforts to help her as hard as she had everyone else but they never gave up.

For a long time, she thought she deserved everything that had happened to her. The abuse, the beatings, the vicious cruelties that children—and sometimes adults—show to anyone weaker than they are.

As far as she knew, she was Katie Golightly, the bastard kid of a junkie and a whore who had basically thrown her away.

After she finally came to trust the Spencers, counseling had helped her shake off that victim mentality. She had worked hard to put those dark, ugly years behind her, to see herself as more than the sum of where she had come from because that was the way the Spencers saw her.

She wasn't sure even the best counseling in the world would help her now.

Her anger was like sulfuric acid eating away at the edges of everything she had worked so hard to become. She had lived through hell not because she'd been born to it but because someone had stolen her away from something else and thrust her into it.

If not for Brenda, she would never have been scavenging through Dumpsters or fighting off fourteen-year-old perverts with a kitchen knife. She would have been safe, happy, loved, living a far different life with the McKinnons.

She couldn't seem to get that image out of her head of a loving father and mother and two older brothers she knew would have fought to the death to protect her.

Brenda had taken all of that from her. Family vacations and Christmas mornings and Fourth of July picnics. She had taken an innocent little girl from her happy life and shoved her into a nightmare, and, damn it, Kate wanted to know why. She *had* to know why.

Maybe then she could finally put that past behind her and move forward.

Chapter 8

Rain found them in Oklahoma and followed them across Arkansas where they had stopped for the night, and now to northern Mississippi.

Kate didn't mind. She found the steady, hypnotic rhythm of the windshield wipers and the rain sluicing under their tires soothing, relaxing. It was almost cozy driving along through the rain, safe and warm in their car with B. B. King and Buddy Guy wailing out the blues on the stereo.

"Good choice," Hunter had said when she'd dug through her CD collection for her favorite bluesmen that morning when they'd passed the Arkansas state line an hour or so earlier.

"We have to listen to the blues in Mississippi. I think it's the law."

"If it's not, it should be," he had answered. She could swear he had almost let loose with a smile that time, but he'd poker-faced it before she could be sure.

He smelled wonderful, as usual—soap and expensive aftershave and just-washed male. In the close confines of the SUV, she couldn't take a breath without inhaling the scent of him. She found it erotic and disturbing at the same time.

What would he do if she closed her eyes for the next few hours, just listening to the rain and the music and filling her senses with his smell?

Oh Kate. What a fine mess you've gotten yourself into.

The ultimate goal of this trip was certainly something she wanted, to make her peace with what had happened to her, or at least to gain understanding. As she had feared, though, she was discovering an unfortunate side effect.

Hunter.

More precisely, her feelings for him.

For all of the five years she had known him, Hunter had been making her pulse skip and her insides quiver. Though she knew it was hopeless—and embarrassing, when it came right down to it—she had long ago accepted the fact that she had a powerful crush on the man.

Now, after more than two days of being with him constantly, she had finally faced the grim, inevitable truth. Her feelings for Hunter Bradshaw ran much deeper than a simple crush.

If she wasn't careful, she would find herself headlong, foolishly in love with the man.

That would be disastrous, she knew. All she would get from him would be a shattered heart. Though there might be some physical attraction stirring between them—and she still wasn't sure whether that had only been one-sided—that was as far as things went.

If anything, her revelations the day before about her life in foster care seemed to have given him a definite disgust of her. After they had talked about her history, he'd said little throughout the afternoon and evening, and had barely made eye contact with her when they'd stopped at a motel off the freeway in Little Rock close to midnight.

She was only glad she hadn't told him the whole of it.

Kate tried not to let his reaction hurt, but she wasn't succeeding very well. With every centimeter he withdrew further into himself, tiny sharp barbs lodged under her skin.

A big baby, that's what you are, she chided herself. *The man is doing you a huge favor. He doesn't need you making a fool of yourself over him.*

Still, as they drove southeast across northern Mississippi with rain clicking against the windshield, she listened to B.B.'s mournful guitar and you-treat-me-bad songs and thought she could write a few pretty decent blues songs of her own right about now.

"Belle is probably ready for a run to work off her breakfast," Hunter said after only a few hours on the road. "Thought I'd stop in Tupelo for gas."

"Great. I need to stretch my legs too. At least the rain looks like it's letting up."

By the time they took the exit east of town, the rain had slowed to a drizzle, then stopped altogether.

Hunter pulled up to the pump at a busy truck stop. Really busy, Kate thought. The convenience store inside was full of people, about twenty or so. She wondered at it until she saw a Greyhound bus pulled up to one of the diesel pumps on the other side of the building.

By now, she knew the drill. He started to fill up the tank while she opened the cargo door, hooked the leash on the dog and let her out of her crate.

Hunter scanned the bustle of activity inside. "There might be a wait if you need to use the restroom."

"I'm good. I'll just take Belle for a little walk around the block. We'll be back in a minute."

"Be careful. It looks like a safe enough neighborhood, but you never know."

She mustered a smile. "I'll keep my guard up, Detective."

She was warmed by his concern, even though she knew he was the kind of man who would show that same solicitude to anyone. Tempting as it was, she couldn't let herself read anything more into it.

She walked away from the truck stop and took off down a small cluster of businesses. The air was cool and misty, but she didn't mind. Compared to the bone-numbing cold of the Utah December they had left, she found this milder weather refreshing.

Belle kept up a fast clip as they walked through the largely industrial area. Kate didn't mind that either—her cramped muscles welcomed the activity. Maybe a little vigorous exercise would take her mind off the futility of her feelings for Hunter.

A few more days, she thought. They would probably reach Miami late that night or the next morning. If all went well, they would find Brenda quickly, shake some answers out of her and then be back in Utah by the end of the week.

She would be ready for her next rotation, Hunter would figure out what he wanted to do with the rest of his life, and their paths would probably rarely intersect, only through their connections to Taylor and Wyatt.

Her hand tightened on the leash and she forced herself to keep walking, even though she suddenly wanted to stop and have a good cry.

When they were about half a block from the truck stop, Belle suddenly spied a convenient tree at the mouth of an alley. As Kate slowed to wait for the dog to mark territory she would likely never see again, she heard voices and saw a trio of people standing a dozen yards away.

An older black man was deep in conversation with a couple of white boys who looked to be about fifteen.

She raised a hand in greeting and was about to say a polite good morning when Hunter's words echoed in her mind. *Be careful.* Something didn't sit right about the scene. She couldn't quite put a finger on what—maybe just a subtle vibrating tension in the air.

The three hadn't noticed her yet. She was going to keep on walking when Belle suddenly growled low in her throat, something so rare for the dog that for a moment Kate could only stare.

She shifted her gaze back to the group down the alley at the same moment the sun found a thin spot in the heavy layer of dank gray clouds. A shaft of light caught on the men and flashed off something silvery in one of the boy's hands.

A knife! One of the boys was holding it close to the man's side!

Kate caught her breath; her fingers tangled in Belle's leash. Every instinct urged her just to keep walking. This was not her business and the last thing she needed right now was to jump into the middle of somebody else's trouble. She had plenty of her own to deal with.

Even as she thought it, she knew she couldn't walk away. Two young, muscled, shaved-head little punks against one frail old man just wasn't fair, and the tough little scrapper she'd been at seven urged her to help even up the odds.

The smaller teen must have heard Belle's growl. He turned, a triple row of earrings swaying in his ear. He looked tough and wiry, with a pierced lip and a jagged scar above one eyebrow.

He nudged the other boy—the one with the knife—who

shifted his gaze from the old man to her, his eyes small and mean.

Unlike his companion, this one had no earrings or scars, but a tattoo of a hissing snake slithered up his neck, the forked tongue licking his jawbone.

They both looked rough and scary, though she saw they were heartbreakingly young, maybe only fourteen or fifteen.

For just a moment, Kate stood in the alley, her nerves buzzing and her mind working frantically to come up with a plan. She had to do something and fast, so she went with the first thing that came to her.

"There you are!" She stepped into the alley, dragging a bristling Belle along with her. "Where have you been?"

As she continued moving toward them, all three males looked at her as if fireworks had just started shooting out of the top of her head.

"We've been looking everywhere for you!"

She reached for the elderly man's elbow as if he were her best friend. He was bony and slight and she wanted to punch both of these little punks for terrorizing an old man.

"Come on, let's get some lunch," she said to the stranger. "You know how your blood sugar dips if you don't eat on a regular schedule."

The man frowned in her direction though his eyes didn't make contact with hers. As soon as he stepped away from the building with a baffled kind of look, she realized why. In the heat of the moment, she had missed the white-tipped cane resting at his feet.

He was blind!

All the more reason to intervene. What kind of evil spawn preyed on a blind man? She reached for the cane, shaking with the urge to whack these two young delinquents over the head with it.

One of the teens—Snake Boy—slid a combat boot over the cane so she couldn't pick it up. "Stay out of this, lady. This ain't none of your business."

"What isn't? I'm just here to take my friend back to the car."

"Don't try to play us, bitch. He ain't your friend. He walked off the Greyhound, same as we did. You weren't nowhere on there." His cold eyes scoured her from head to toe, a suddenly dangerous light in them. "Believe me, I'd a noticed a li'l hot thing like you."

Now what? Even as adrenaline pumped through her, her mind felt slow and dull. "Um, we were meeting up here to take him with us the rest of the way. Come on, Grandpa."

The two punks seemed to think that was the funniest thing they'd ever heard. "Here that, old man?" Snake Boy said. "This little white girl says you're her grandpa."

"Hi honey." The blind man smiled in her direction. "I was wondering when you'd get here."

Charmed by him and grateful he was willing to play along, Kate smiled even though she knew he couldn't see it. She tucked his arm firmly in hers. "I'm right here. Now let's go on and get some lunch. I know how you love that chicken-fried steak they serve at our special place."

She started to drag him toward the street, hoping sheer cojones would get them out of the alley, but the boys weren't having any of it.

The twitchy little one stepped forward and grabbed the man's other arm. He produced a knife of his own and Kate's heart sank.

She had an awful feeling that two tough punks with knives against a woman, a dog and a blind man wasn't a scenario that was likely going to end happily.

"You ain't going anywhere, Grandpa, until you hand over that roll we saw you flashin' around back there."

"Okay. Okay. I'll give you what you want. Just don't hurt the young lady here."

"You ain't calling the shots here, Grandpa. We're the ones with the pig stickers." As if to emphasize his point, Snake Boy started to grab for Kate.

Kate wasn't exactly sure what happened next. Belle barked, protective of her, as Kate tried to wrench her arm out of the punk's grasp. In the confusion, the elderly gentleman stumbled a little—right into the nervous boy holding the knife.

He grunted with pain then staggered and fell to the ground. Kate took a lurching step forward, a strangled cry in her throat and her hold on the leash going slack.

Belle took advantage of her newfound freedom and escaped the thick tension between humans, running out of the alley with her leash trailing behind her like the tail of a comet.

Panic spurted through Kate as she rushed to the fallen man but she did her best to push it away. She had to keep a level head. One of the first lessons in med school was how to stay calm in a crisis.

The kid holding the bloody knife looked like he was about to cry. "Damn! I didn't mean to stick the old dude! He fell right into my knife."

"His own frigging fault." Snake Boy scratched his tattoo, his eyes cold. "If he'd a just handed over his stash, everything would have been cool."

She would have expected them to take off but they loitered there in the alley as if not quite sure what direction to run, while she assessed the man's injuries.

Kate pulled the elderly man's crisp blue dress shirt from his slacks and lifted it free of the wound, a two-inch puncture just below his rib cage. She had just finished her rotation in the emergency room of a level-one trauma center. Stab wounds had been an everyday occurrence and this one looked cleaner than most.

The old man grimaced as she probed the wound. To her relief, it looked as if the knife had glanced off the rib.

She didn't think he would have any internal injuries, but the wound was bleeding copiously.

"Kid made a mess of my best suit," the man said in a disgusted voice. "I'm probably bleeding all over it, aren't I?"

"We want to help you keep as much of your blood as possible inside, for your sake and for your suit's. I'll do my best to keep the damage to a minimum," she promised.

"One of you will have to go for help," she told the teens. "We need an ambulance to take Mr...." She stopped, realizing she didn't know the man's name. "To take my grandpa here to the hospital."

Snake Boy raised an eyebrow. "You can forget that, lady. We're out of here."

"You might want to reconsider that."

The deep voice from the alley's mouth was the most welcome sound in the world. She looked up from applying a makeshift pressure bandage from her sweater to find Hunter standing there, Belle right behind him. *Good girl,* she thought. *Way to go for reinforcements.*

As the cavalry, Hunter was perfect. He had never seemed so big, so mean, so dangerous.

"Screw this." Snake Boy didn't look intimidated. "Come on, Juice."

Hunter moved farther into the alley and, for the first time, Kate noticed he carried a gun.

"Like I said—" his voice was as dark and as deadly as the gun that had suddenly appeared in his hand "—you might want to reconsider."

The smaller boy again looked like he was just an earring away from bawling, but the older one just looked resigned.

"You a cop?"

"Used to be."

Snake closed his eyes and gritted out a raw epithet that would have singed Kate's eyebrows if she hadn't spent plenty of time in an E.R., hearing much worse than this gangsta wannabe could ever hope to dish out.

"Watch your mouth," her patient said from the ground. "There's a lady present."

With the gun pointed at the two juvenile delinquents, Hunter fished out his cell phone and dialed 911 to report the armed robbery and assault.

"An ambulance is on the way," he told them, after he'd summed up the situation and given their location in a brisk, efficient way, which said better than anything else that he still had plenty of cop left in him.

"What a bother. I don't need an ambulance." The older man's voice was smooth, well-modulated, with only a slight southern accent. "He barely nicked me. I've done worse than this shaving."

Hunter looked to Kate for confirmation, but she shook her head.

"I'm sorry, Mr...."

She knew he must be in pain but he still mustered a smile. "Mr. Henry Monroe, miss."

Charmed again by his polite manners, she smiled back. "I'm Kate Spencer and this is Hunter Bradshaw. Mr. Monroe, I'm sorry but you've got a deep puncture wound that's going to need several layers of stitches. I don't think they'll have to operate but you need to be treated at a hospital."

He appeared to digest this information for a moment but it didn't sway him. "Well, now, I appreciate your help, miss, but if I don't get back to that gas station in a real hurry, I'm afraid I'll miss the Greyhound. My granddaughter is dancing in *The Nutcracker* tonight in Memphis and I decided to ride up and surprise her."

"We'll find you another bus," Kate promised. "Don't worry, we'll make sure you get to Memphis, won't we Hunter?"

As sirens wailed in the distance, Hunter shifted his gaze from the two punks at the business end of his gun to her.

He gave her a long, inscrutable look out of eyes, the color of a stormy sky, then he shook his head and she could swear she saw one corner of his mouth turn up and amusement flicker in those dark eyes. "Sure we will, Mr. Monroe. Don't worry about a thing."

A squad car pulled up with a couple of Tupelo's finest before she could say anything else and Kate turned her attention back to her patient.

Hunter leaned back in the uncomfortable chair in the E.R. waiting room of the Tupelo hospital and surveyed Kate in the chair across from him.

She had bloodstains on her shirt, her hair had slipped free of the casual ponytail she'd pulled it into that morning and her makeup had washed away in the drizzle that had descended on them while they were trying to get Mr. Monroe into the ambulance.

She looked bedraggled and tired and worried, and he had to just about sit on his hands to keep from reaching for her.

How was it that she seemed to grow more beautiful with every moment they spent together? Physically, yes, he had always thought her attractive. Even without makeup her features were elegant, soft and lovely like a woman in an old-world painting.

But more than that, *she* was beautiful, deep inside where the rest of the world couldn't see. She had faced down two little dumb-ass punks to protect an elderly blind man with nothing more than her own courage—and now she refused to leave the hospital until they made sure she found the man's treatment acceptable.

"It took three layers of stitches but everything's closed up tight now. They're just bandaging him up but I thought I'd better come find you to give you a status report," she said.

"I appreciate that. You know, I didn't realize part of our trip itinerary was a tour of hospitals across the country," he couldn't resist adding.

She made a face. "I'm sorry. I had to come along. I don't suppose it makes sense to you but in a way Mr. Monroe feels like a patient of mine. I couldn't just leave him alone in a strange city."

As someone who used to have the same level of caring about his own job, he had to admire her dedication to her chosen profession; at the same time, part of him seethed with envy. How long had it been since he'd cared about anything that passionately? He couldn't remember—and he wasn't sure he ever would again.

"Are they keeping him overnight, then?"

"The attending physician is pushing hard for it. He seems like a bit of a jerk. But Mr. Monroe is a stubborn one—he insists he's got to leave. *The Nutcracker* is waiting."

Hunter studied her. "You want to take him to Memphis, don't you?"

A hint of color dusted her cheekbones and she gave him a sheepish look. "The thought had occurred to me," she admitted. "I just don't feel good about sending him off alone on a Greyhound with his injury. If I really were his doctor, I would order him to bed for a few days but I don't think he would take that advice."

"You do realize Memphis is more than two hundred miles out of our way round trip, right?"

She fretted with a loose thread on her sweater. "Yes. And you've already done so much for me, I know I can't ask this of you, too. I don't know, maybe I could call the daughter and have her come get him."

"Would she have time to drive down here and still make it back in time for the granddaughter's performance?"

"Probably not." She fell quiet. "I'm willing to entertain other suggestions if you have any."

He wondered if Kate was even aware of her habit of collecting strays. Mariah, Henry. Himself. She tried her best to heal the whole world, whether they wanted healing or were content to stay mired in the muck of their own angst.

Was it because she'd been a stray herself? Because she knew what it was like to be lost and alone and hurting and she couldn't stand to see anyone else in that condition?

Two hundred more miles meant at least three more hours with her. A hundred-eighty more minutes for her to wrap her fingers around his heart and keep tugging it out of the cold, dark corner he'd shoved it into after Dru's murder and his arrest.

He sighed. "What's two hundred miles when we've already come this far?"

Chapter 9

"So there I was, blind as a bat, stubborn as a one-eyed mule and stuck out in that fishing boat with no idea which way to row toward shore." Henry Monroe, seated in the back where he could theoretically stretch out, guffawed a little.

Despite the blood covering his shirt and the heavily bandaged abdomen Hunter knew was underneath that shirt, Henry sat up straight as an ironing board and never lost his smile the entire drive from Tupelo. It seemed as permanent on his features as that punk kid's hissing viper tattoo.

"Let me tell you," he went on, "I did some mighty serious praying that day. Turns out God *does* listen to stubborn old fools who ought to know better. Next thing I knew that fishing boat was touching bottom and I was touching dry land. That was the last time I tried that, you can be sure. I still go fishing but I now force myself to have the patience to wait until my good friend Lamont Beauvais can go along. He doesn't hear too well and I don't see too well so between the two of us we make a pretty fine team."

Kate's laughter bubbled through the vehicle like a spring deep in the mountains—sweet and clear and refreshing.

Hunter loved listening to that sound. It seemed to seep through all the bloody cracks in his soul like healing balm.

He hadn't heard her laugh in a long time—not a real one, anyway, the kind of deep laugh that started low in the pit of the stomach and burst out like water from an uncapped irrigation pipe.

Amazing how one elderly man with a vision impairment and a cheerful smile could lighten the mood in the SUV so dramatically.

He wasn't sure he had fully recognized how strained things were between him and Kate, the finely tuned tension always humming under their polite conversation, until Henry Monroe climbed in the back seat at that hospital parking lot and set about shaking things up.

He only wished they could take Henry along the rest of the way to Florida with them, but they were only about twenty minutes from Memphis and his daughter's house.

Henry and Kate had gotten along like a house on fire. During the hundred-mile journey from Tupelo to Memphis, Hunter had listened while Henry told her about his life as a Baptist preacher and how his macular degeneration didn't stop him from tending to his flock.

Kate, in turn, had told him the reason for their journey, about the stunning discovery six weeks earlier about her kidnapping, that everything she thought she knew about herself and her life had been a lie and how they were on a quest for answers.

Hunter had mostly been an observer to their conversation.

Nothing new in that, he thought, suddenly realizing how detached he had been from life in the last three years.

Maybe it had been a form of self-preservation, the only way he had of protecting anything good and decent left inside him, but he had somehow distanced himself from the events that had turned his life upside down.

From the moment of his arrest for the murders of Dru and Mickie, he had retreated to a safe, private place inside his psyche. He was only coming to realize on this journey that a part of him was still inside that place peeking around the corner, afraid to venture out even though he knew the coast was clear.

"That fishing trip was in the early days after my vision started going south, when I was still fighting and bucking against fate. I've become a lot smarter since I hit seventy."

Kate smiled but her eyes were serious. "It must have been difficult for you at first."

"Oh, it was. I was angry for a long time. I fought against it as long as I could, held onto my driver's license long after I could safely drive. That was the worst, giving that up. I still miss taking off in my old Mercury and driving for hours down country roads."

In the rearview mirror, Hunter saw him shake his head. "I spent many a night on my knees crying out to God, asking why I was being punished so. First he took my wife Eleanor, then he took my vision so I couldn't even see the faces of the children and grandchildren my Ellie left behind. It seemed a mighty cruel trick to play on a man who had tried to spend his whole life in service to him."

Hunter thought of the long nights in prison when he had cried out to anyone who might be listening. He too had felt forsaken, forgotten. Prison is hell for an innocent man and day by day his faith had dwindled. He wasn't sure now that he could ever find it again.

"What changed?" he asked suddenly, earning a surprised look from Kate. "You seem to have accepted your condition now. How did that happen?"

In the mirror, he could see Henry's soft smile. "I realized I had two choices. I could sit there in my house until I died, scared and angry and bitter. Or I could go on living. I decided to go on."

That's what Hunter hadn't done, he realized. He had been out of Point of the Mountain for six weeks but his bitterness against Martin James for what he had done was keeping him in another kind of prison, one with bars just as strong.

He would stay there, hiding inside his anger and betrayal, until he made the choice to go on living.

He wasn't sure he could. After three years of believing he would be executed, he was finding the transition to contemplating a future a little difficult to maneuver.

He was still lost in thought as they drove the rest of the way to the comfortable suburban neighborhood where Henry directed them.

"It's a mighty kind thing you folks have done here, driving me all this way," Henry said as they neared his daughter's home.

He wasn't kind at all, Hunter thought. He just couldn't say no to Kate Spencer.

"We're happy to do it, aren't we, Hunter?" she said.

Just hearing her say his name shouldn't send heat trickling down his spine like the rain dripping down the windshield, but there it was.

"Right," he murmured.

"I can't thank you enough. I'd have been in a real fix if you all hadn't come along when you did."

Kate smiled. "I'm just glad we were there to help."

"Is this the right place?" Hunter asked as he pulled up in front of the address Henry had given. "It's a white house with green shutters and a tire swing in a big maple."

"That's the one."

Hunter pulled into the driveway. He turned off the Jeep then climbed out and opened the passenger door to help Henry from the back seat.

He wasn't at all surprised when Kate climbed out too and came around to offer her other arm.

"Oh now, you don't have to mollycoddle me. I'm just fine."

"I want to talk to your daughter about caring for your injury," she said firmly.

They made quite a trio, Hunter thought as they made their way with slow care through the light drizzle to the front porch hung with garlands of fragrant pine.

Henry rang the doorbell and a few moments later a young woman with long bead-tipped braids and a harried expression opened the door, sending out a rush of warm air that smelled of gingerbread and cinnamon and sugar cookies.

A coltish little girl about eight with Henry's warm eyes peeked around her.

Hunter decided the whole detour was worth it to see the stunned glee in the little girl's eyes.

"Grandpa! You came! You came!"

She rushed to throw her arms around Henry, something that would undoubtedly have been painful with his injuries, but Kate stepped in front of him first.

"Grandpa, you're bleeding!" the little girl said, her voice suddenly fearful. "What happened?"

The daughter's eyes were wide with shock. "Dad? What are you doing here? Who are these people? What's going on?"

"I came to see *The Nutcracker*. I couldn't miss my little Antonia. On the way I was in a little accident but I'm fine. Just fine. Don't you worry, Raquel. My friends Hunter and Katie here helped me out and offered to give me a ride from Tupelo."

"What kind of accident?"

"Now that's a long story. The important thing is I'm fine and I made it here. I may need to borrow one of Marcus's shirts, though. I'm afraid this one is beyond saving."

He bent to his granddaughter. "I see pink. Are you wearing your costume? You're going to have to tell me all about it."

Antonia dragged him over to the couch and started describing her frothy tulle costume. Hunter didn't miss the way Kate made sure he was settled before turning back to the daughter.

In her calm, clinical way, she described the attempted mugging and Henry's subsequent injury, assuring Raquel quickly that his injury wasn't serious.

She then gave the woman Henry's hospital discharge papers and explained the care his wound would need.

The daughter was effusive in her gratitude for what they had done. She insisted on sending them on their way with two huge bags of home-baked goodies—several kinds of holiday cookies, a tin of fudge and thick gingerbread.

Finally, they said their goodbyes, again with Kate leaving her contact information and insisting Henry e-mail her and let her know how his wound was healing.

At the rate she was acquiring her strays, she would have e-mail penpals across the country.

Though they urged him to rest, Henry insisted on walking them to the door. He shook Hunter's hand solemnly, then hugged Kate.

"I hope you find the answers you need," he said, those

blind eyes filled with more wisdom and serenity than Hunter could ever hope to gain. "Both of you."

With that advice, they walked out into the cold drizzle.

Kate didn't know what kind of magic wand Henry Monroe had waved inside at Hunter before they dropped him in Memphis, but whatever Baptist-minister voodoo he'd whipped up packed a heck of a punch.

Hunter seemed like a completely different man than the one she had traveled with for three days. He seemed younger, somehow. Lighter.

He had smiled more on the stretch of road between Memphis and Atlanta than he had the entire trip and she could swear she'd even heard him laugh once, though it had been so fleeting she couldn't be a hundred percent sure.

How long had it been since she had seen him like this? she wondered. Probably since before his arrest. No, before he became tangled up with Dru Ferrin and her lies.

She wasn't sure what had caused the big change and she couldn't take the time to figure it out—not when it was taking every iota of her strength to protect her heart from this version of Hunter Bradshaw.

She had a tough enough time trying to resist him at his most terse and moody. This relaxed, teasing man was positively dangerous.

Maybe the magic taking away that haunted look in his eyes had something to do with Raquel Monroe-Payton's fudge. Hunter certainly seemed to be enjoying it.

He grabbed for another piece out of the tin, then made a face. "Sorry. I'm being a pig, aren't I?"

"Eat it all. I'm not a big fan."

"I am. Always have been. In fact, I dreamed of fudge in prison. That sounds really stupid, doesn't it?"

She laughed a little but shook her head.

"Yeah, it does," he said. "After my mother died, we had this housekeeper who made this absolutely incredible fudge. Real butter, walnuts, the works. I think she sold her recipe to one of the big Salt Lake candy companies. Made a fortune. Anyway, she used to make it for Taylor and me whenever we were upset about something. A punishment from the Judge, a bad grade on a test. A particularly bad day when we were missing having a mother. Whatever. Helen McKay's fudge is exactly what I think of when I hear the words *comfort food*."

If ever there was a time he had needed solace, it was during his prison time, she thought. "You should have told Taylor about your craving," she said. "I'm sure she would have moved heaven and earth to keep you permanently supplied."

"It was hard to admit I needed anything," he said, his voice low.

In that moment, with the soft rain falling on the roof and the smell of leather seats and fudge and Hunter surrounding her, Kate faced the truth.

She had worried earlier that morning about trying to protect her heart from him, but the damage was already done. This was no silly schoolgirl crush.

She was in love with him. She suddenly realized that she had been for a long time, probably as long as she'd known him. She loved his honor, she loved his strength, she loved the small kindnesses he always seemed a little abashed to show.

"Kate? Everything okay?"

She fought the urge to press a hand to her feckless, destined-for-disaster heart. "Um, fine," she lied. "Great. Why do you ask?"

"You just looked a little funny there for a minute. Are you a little carsick? Need me to stop?"

"No. I'm fine."

Though he still looked concerned, Hunter let the subject rest. Kate gazed out the windshield, her thoughts whirling. What was she supposed to do with this information now? Her first instinct was to tell him to drop her off at the next airport so she could catch a flight home. Even as the thought whispered in her mind, she discarded it. She couldn't do that. She had to stick this out, no matter how difficult the road.

Maybe she shouldn't be looking at this time together as torture, she thought, but as an opportunity to store up as many memories as possible. After this trip, they would go their separate ways, but for the next several days at least, he was hers.

Her cell phone bleeped just as she drifted off to sleep in a hotel room that seemed to whirl around a little like she was still riding shotgun in Hunter's Jeep.

Kate thought about ignoring the blasted thing. In the chaos of their quick trip, she had forgotten all about it in the bottom of her purse until she went digging through for a business card to leave for Henry. Now she wished she'd left it off.

It bleeped again, vibrating on the bedside table like a tiny angry cat. The temptation just to let it ring was overwhelming, but then she thought of the dozen messages she had yet to check and sighed.

She had ignored real life for three days, cocooned in Hunter's SUV, loathe for some strange reason to let the world intrude on their quest. What if she'd missed something important?

With another sigh she grabbed it and hit the talk button just before the call would have gone to voice mail.

"Hello?"

"You're there! Oh thank heavens!"

Kate heard Lynn McKinnon's soft, cultured voice on the other end and let out a long breath, wishing she had followed her instincts and ignored the call.

"Yes, I'm here."

"Oh Charlotte." Lynn paused slightly and Kate could picture her mother's fair skin turning rosy with embarrassment. "I'm sorry—Kate. Drat. I keep trying to think of you as Kate but it's hard after so many years of you being our Charley. I'm sorry."

"It's all right. I know who you mean."

"Thank you, darling. Anyway, I'm so glad I finally caught you. I've been worried sick! I've been trying to reach you for days!"

Kate lay back on the bed and closed her eyes, unused to the guilt that pinched at her with sharp aggravating fingers.

"I'm sorry," she said again. "My cell phone has been off for a few days and I only realized it this afternoon. I haven't had time to check messages. Is everything okay?"

"Yes. Everything's fine. Now I feel silly for worrying about you. It's just that I was in the city Monday for a little last-minute Christmas shopping and stopped by your apartment to see if you might like to have lunch since you weren't working."

"Oh?"

"Your car was in the parking lot but your next-door neighbor said she hadn't seen you around for a few days."

Lynn fell silent, obviously waiting for some kind of explanation for the anomaly. She should have told her family what she was doing, Kate realized. She was embarrassed and a little ashamed that the idea of vetting her travel plans past them had never even occurred to her.

"I'm not trying to crowd you or anything," Lynn said after an awkward pause. "You don't have to report your every move to me. I suppose I'm a little paranoid. We've only just found you and I can't bear the thought of losing you again."

Thick emotion rose in her throat as Kate heard the concern in Lynn's voice. She wanted so much to be able to accept the love this woman and the rest of her family stood ready to embrace her with. But she felt as if her hate and bitterness formed a heavy magnetic shield around her like something out of a science-fiction movie, repelling any of the McKinnons' attempts to reach out to her.

"I'm sorry. I should have told you where I was going. I'm in Florida."

"Florida!" Lynn's voice sounded as shocked as if Kate had announced she was trapped deep in the Congo. "My goodness! You didn't say anything about a trip Saturday night at the wedding. Or did I just miss it somehow?"

"You didn't miss anything. This was a spur-of-the-moment thing." She hesitated to tell Lynn the reason for the trip, then decided there was no reason to prevaricate. "I'm looking for answers to my past. I'm hoping to find Brenda Golightly, the woman I thought was my mother until six weeks ago when Wyatt and Gage found me."

There was dead silence on the other end, stretching out so long Kate wondered if she'd lost the connection. She was afraid she had hurt the other woman by her announcement, but when Lynn spoke, all Kate could hear in her voice was concern and a love so clear and pure, her eyes started to burn.

"Oh sweetheart. Are you sure this is something you want to do?"

Kate blinked away the tears that threatened but her eyes still stung. "I don't want to. Not really. Until a month ago, I would have been happy never seeing her again."

Lynn made a distressed kind of sound. Kate hadn't told the McKinnons much about her life with Brenda, only that she had been taken away from her and put into foster care when she was seven.

She thought the grim reality would be too painful for them to hear. Most parents want their children to have lovely, shiny-bright childhoods, free of darkness or despair. Hers was tarnished and grim and she hadn't wanted to burden the McKinnons with any of the details.

She had the unsettling thought as she lay on that hotel bed with the cell phone to her ear that maybe that was one of the ways she kept them at arm's length. If they didn't know what she'd lived through, they didn't really know *her*.

"I have so much anger inside me," she confessed to Lynn, with an odd feeling that she had just stretched out a bridge of sorts. "I need to know why me. And right now Brenda is the only person who might have the answer to that."

Lynn was quiet for a long moment. "I wish you had told me were going. Maybe I could have come with you. Or Sam or one of your brothers. You have endured so much alone. I hate the idea of you going through this by yourself too."

"I'm not alone," she assured her. She rose and wandered to the window, restless suddenly. "Hunter came with me."

"Taylor's brother? That Hunter?"

"Yes."

There was another awkward silence then a long, drawn out "Ohhhh."

Kate flushed at the speculation she heard in Lynn's voice but didn't correct her.

"Have you spoken to her yet? To this Brenda person?"

Kate gazed out at the courtyard below. Her room faced the swimming pool and the pool lights glowed green in the night.

"No. We're only in Jacksonville. The last I heard of Brenda, she was in Miami so that's where we've decided to start. We should be there tomorrow. I believe she had a sister there we're going to try to contact but for all I know, this is a wild goose chase. She's probably halfway across the country."

Wouldn't she feel horrible if, after all this effort and energy, they couldn't find Brenda at all? She would be mortified if she'd dragged Hunter all this way for nothing.

"Did you talk to Gage about what you're doing?" Lynn asked.

Kate thought of her oldest brother, the FBI agent. Of all the members of her newly discovered family, she found Gage hardest to read. Sam, her father, seemed quiet and steady. He worked with his hands but he still had a bright mind and a deep calmness about him.

Lynn was open and sincere, eager for Kate to love her.

She knew it wouldn't be hard to care for Wyatt—he was her best friend's husband now and she would have loved him for that alone, but he had earned a special place in her heart for helping to free Hunter.

Gage, though, was still a mystery to her. He was abrupt to the point of reticence but he obviously adored his new wife and daughters, and Kate had seen moments of great sweetness between the four of them.

Kate knew Gage and Wyatt had never given up finding her and she had learned enough about the FBI agent in the past month to guess that her disappearance probably contributed at least in part to his career choice.

"No," she said now to Lynn. "I didn't talk to anyone but Hunter."

"Your case is still technically open. Gage may have some information on this woman's whereabouts."

Of all the members of her family, he had been the one most interested in details about her childhood as Katie Golightly and the woman she had believed to be her mother.

"Do you think he's still working the case?"

Her mother sighed. "If I know my oldest son, I have no doubt whatsoever. Even though we've found you again, Gage won't be able to rest until he finds out why you were taken and by whom."

Maybe she was more like her brother than she thought. "I need that too. That's why we're here."

"I'll talk to Gage. He may have some information that could be helpful to you."

"Thank you."

Kate didn't know what to say after that. She hated this distance, this awkwardness she always felt when talking to Lynn, and wondered if it would ever ease.

"I'm so glad I finally reached you," Lynn said after moment. "I know it's silly but I'll sleep easier tonight. Will you forgive me for panicking?"

"Of course."

They said their goodbyes, with Lynn's repeated promise to talk to Gage, then Kate hung up her phone. She set it carefully on the dresser, then opened the sliding doors to the small terrace of her room, suddenly desperate for air.

The night was lovely, clear and comfortable. Kate wandered to the railing, gazing out at the garden around the pool. Though still just off the freeway, this was a better scale of hotel than they'd stayed in yet on this journey, with an extravagant pool and lush landscaping, complete with twinkling little Christmas lights in the palm trees.

She and Brenda never would have stayed in a place like this. Their accommodations were usually the kind of scary, hole-in-the-wall motel that had shifty-eyed clerks, card-board-thin walls and bedsprings that creaked.

Kate would usually make a bed for herself on the bath-room floor and curl up while Brenda entertained a gentle-man friend in the other room or would pass out on the bed.

Most of the time, she doubted whether Brenda knew— or cared—that Kate was even there.

Kate thought of Lynn McKinnon's loving concern, and the stark contrast between what should have been and what was brought those tears she had been fighting to the surface again. This time she couldn't stop them and they burst free.

She stood there for a long time with the moist breeze ed-dying around her and tears trickling down her cheeks.

She didn't realize she was no longer alone until Hunter spoke from the balcony next to hers.

"In prison, nights were the worst. During the day you could wear a facade of indifference. But at night we were all locked into our cells, alone with only the guilt to taunt and torment us. Those of us who didn't have guilt had nothing left but our fear."

"I'm sorry." She sniffled, embarrassed at herself for let-ting her emotions out.

"Don't be. Nothing wrong with crying."

"It's either cry or scream right now. And I'm afraid if I start screaming, I won't stop. I don't know what to do with this anger. I can lock it away for long stretches of time but some-times no matter how hard I try to keep it contained my hate and bitterness bursts free and I can't think about anything else."

"Are you angry? Or are you just hurting?"

She gave a ragged-sounding laugh. "Both."

Only about two feet separated their terraces. Before Kate realized what he intended, Hunter grabbed his railing and

swung his body over to her terrace with an agility that left
her blinking.

It was a crazy thing to do, he thought, but he couldn't bear
her crying over there by herself. He leaned with her on the
railing, gazing out at the twinkling palm trees and the bou-
gainvillea and the deep green of the pool lights.

The cool breeze lifted his hair and Hunter thought how
odd it was that three days earlier they had stood together on
the deck of his canyon home while he'd watched her catch
snowflakes on her tongue.

"What let it out this time?" he asked quietly. "Your hurt
or anger or whatever it is?"

In the moonlight, he saw her chin quiver a little but she
quickly straightened it out again.

"Lynn McKinnon just called me. My mother." Her laugh
was short and bitter. "My *mother*. I can't even say the word.
The woman has loved me for twenty-six years—never gave
up hope of finding me again—and I can't even do her the
courtesy of calling her by her rightful title. She's a stranger
to me. A stranger I seem to be doing my damnedest to keep
at arm's length."

"Give yourself time. You can't expect to love the McKinnons as if you spent your whole life with them. They understand that. From what I've seen of them, they're decent
people. I'm sure they'll give you whatever space you need
until you're comfortable with them."

"What if that day never comes?"

He couldn't bear the murky pain in her eyes, the heartache threading through her voice. Though he knew it wasn't
the wisest of ideas, he reached for her.

She was stiff with surprise for just a moment before she
sighed and settled against him, small and fragile.

"It will," he murmured. "And if you can never love the

McKinnons as the daughter and sister they lost, you can at least learn to care about them as good, kind people with your best interests at heart."

She said nothing, only settled closer against him. Hunter's arms tightened and he was stunned by the tenderness welling up inside him.

He cleared his throat and continued. "You didn't have them for a big part of your life and that really stinks. But you have them now. That has to count for something, doesn't it? It's more than you had two months ago, more than a lot of people will ever have."

She rested her cheek against his chest, where he was certain she could hear his heart pounding away. "You're right. Intellectually I know you're right. I feel horribly guilty that I can't just lighten up and accept that my life has suddenly taken a bizarre turn. Just be grateful for what I have. But my time with Brenda and…and what came after was awful. Something no child should have to live through. Talking with Lynn just made me contrast what those early years should have been like with the ugly reality."

"I'm sorry, Kate. I wish I could change it for you."

"Contrary to what you must think right now after I just blubbered all over you, this trip is helping. Even if we never find Brenda, being away from the situation has given me a little perspective."

She lifted her face, tearstained but heartbreakingly beautiful in the moonlight. "I think you've got a brilliant future in the damsel-rescuing business."

He mustered a smile, even though it took every ounce of strength he possessed not to kiss her.

Though he was definitely rusty at it, he tried a joke. "Thanks. We're a full-service operation. Finder of lost souls, chauffeur of stranded crime victims, and shoulder to cry on. It's all part of the package."

She smiled and hugged him tighter and Hunter had to clamp his teeth together to hold in his moan of sheer wonder at how good it felt to hold this warm, soft woman.

"Thank you, on all counts," she murmured. "You're very good at what you do."

The pay might be lousy but the benefits sure as hell rocked, he thought.

After a moment, he tried to carefully extricate himself from her arms before he embarrassed both of them by enjoying her touch a little *too* much, but it was like trying to slip out of a warm feather bed on a cold January morning.

He managed to pull one arm away but the other one, curved around her shoulders, refused to budge. While he was trying to remind it who was boss, Kate lifted her face to his again.

In the moonlight, her eyes looked fathomless, deep pools of emotions he couldn't even begin to guess at. She studied him for several heartbeats, then drew in a deep breath, which unfortunately had the side effect of lifting her breasts in even closer contact to his chest. He was trying to keep control and remove the other arm when she spoke, her voice low, throaty.

"Would you kiss me again?"

Every synapse snapped to attention and blood gushed to his groin. "I, uh, don't think that's a very good idea right now."

She gazed at him. "Why not?"

He decided he had no option left but stark honesty. "I haven't been with a woman in three years, Kate. If I kiss you right now, I'm afraid I'll eat you alive."

She appeared to digest his words for a long moment, then she smiled. "And you see this as a problem because…?"

Chapter 10

For the space of about two heartbeats, Hunter managed to resist that look in her eyes, the invitation in her voice, then with a groan he surrendered and dragged her against him, his mouth descending with raw, unbridled hunger.

He wasn't gentle. He swept his tongue inside her mouth and pressed her hard against his erection, his body aching with need.

She made a low sound he took for arousal and wrapped her arms around him, her mouth warm and welcoming.

They stood on the balcony locked together for a long time, mouths and bodies tangled together.

All his pent-up need seemed to explode as he kissed her, roaring through him like a wildfire in high winds.

Finally he dragged his mouth away. "We're going to put on a hell of a show if we don't go inside."

She blinked several times, color stealing over her cheek-bones. "Right. You're right."

With hands that fumbled, she slid open the terrace door and led the way into her hotel room. He was afraid to say anything, afraid she might change her mind, but she kept her hand tucked in his while she slid the door shut and straightened the curtains.

When she was done, she turned back to him, her mouth swollen but her eyes bright with desire and something else he couldn't identify.

He made a low, raw sound and pulled her against him, his mouth finding hers again.

He had never been so aroused, so ravenous for a woman's touch. When she slid her hands inside his shirt to spread those small, elegant fingers across the muscles of his back, he shivered.

He ached to touch her, to fill his hands with feminine flesh, but he felt strangely paralyzed, afraid when he did he would lose whatever thin hold he had on his tenuous control.

He brought his hand to her rib cage, just under the cotton of her shirt, but couldn't seem to move it farther. Her skin was incredible, soft and warm and sweetly scented, and he could feel her small, delicate ribs move with each breath.

"Touch me," she commanded softly against his mouth.

His stomach twirling with anticipation, he slid his thumbs up, up until they brushed the undersides of her breasts through the fabric of her bra.

This time she was the one who shivered, a delicate, erotic tremor. He closed his eyes, overwhelmed by the sensations pouring over him. He felt like a randy teenager again, all raging hormones and fumbling hands and stunned disbelief that she was actually letting him go so far.

"Funny thing about three years of celibacy," he said hoarsely. "I feel like this is the first time I've ever done this."

"I know just what you mean," she murmured, a small smile curving her lips.

He puzzled over that remark but didn't have the brain power to figure it out as she arched against his hands. He had to touch her. Really touch her.

To his vast relief, she wore a front-clasp bra and it only took him a moment to work the tricky thing. At least he hadn't forgotten that particular skill. An instant later his fingers were brushing against warm, soft flesh.

Her breath came in short little gasps as he spent what seemed like hours relearning the feel of a woman's body.

Later he had no conscious memory of slipping off her shirt. One moment it was there, the next she stood before him wearing only her unhooked bra hanging free.

She had small, high breasts, her nipples dark against her creamy skin and he devoured the sight as long as he could stand without touching her again.

With nothing in the way now, he lowered his mouth to the slope of first one breast and then the other, then he drew one taut nipple into his mouth. She smelled of hotel soap and vanilla sugar and woman and he couldn't get enough.

She let out a low, ragged sound and buried her hands in his hair while he savored the incredible wonder of exploring a woman's body again.

Not just any woman, he thought. He had had a dozen chances or more since his release for meaningless sex, but he had wanted none of those women. Only Kate, with her big eyes and her soft heart, made him almost frantic with need.

He was going to explode, right now, he thought. His

arousal jutted against the fabric of his Levi's and all he could think about was coming inside her.

Driven by sudden urgency, he yanked his own shirt over his head, then went to work on the metal buttons of her jeans. To his embarrassment, though, his hands were trembling too hard to work them free, and finally her hands stopped his increasingly frustrated efforts.

"Here. Let me."

Seconds later she slid out of her jeans and her panties, until she lay before him on the bed, an exquisite, naked offering.

He couldn't breathe, could only stare, his blood racing and a wild surge of emotion in his chest.

"I'd forgotten how beautiful a woman's body could be," he said hoarsely. "The hollows and curves and dark places. Do you mind if I just stand here for a moment?"

She blinked, her eyes wide. "I…no. Of course not."

Kate tried not to feel self-conscious as he devoured her with hot and hungry eyes. He had warned her he would eat her alive. She just hadn't expected him to do it with his eyes.

He was the beautiful one, she thought, all muscles and sculpted strength. He had always had a powerful body but his years in prison had turned him into something hard and dangerous.

Finally he slipped out of his jeans, then pulled something out of his wallet and tossed it onto the bedside table.

At the sight of that square metallic packet, Kate's insides twitched with a combination of nerves and anticipation.

"You're prepared."

She thought his short laugh had a layer of self-mockery to it. "I bought a jumbo pack when I got out but they've been gathering dust for the last month."

"Why? I'm sure you've had women banging down your door for the chance to, um, bang down your door."

At last he joined her on the bed and she almost forgot the question when he kissed her again.

"I don't know why," he admitted. "I wanted to but I couldn't manage to work up the enthusiasm—or anything else—for anybody. Until you walked out onto that deck three nights ago."

His words slid through her like an intimate caress and her whole body seemed to catch fire.

He kissed her, a slow, deep mating of tongue and mouth. She wrapped her arms around him, her love for him a heavy weight in her chest.

She was doomed to heartbreak with this man. She knew it as surely as she knew the names of every muscle and tendon his mouth and hands explored, but she wouldn't waste this moment worrying about the future.

Right now she would savor this moment and add it to her precious store of memories.

He kissed her deeply, intensely, as if to memorize each centimeter of her mouth, until she was weak and trembling. After years of second and third dates—and nothing more—she had become a bit of a connoisseur of kissing. She had never experienced this wild desperation, the edginess of his mouth on hers, as if he were afraid this was his last kiss and he wanted to make it matter.

While he kissed her, his hands began to wander over those curves and hollows and dark places he had talked about, until she was breathless and near frantic with need.

Finally, when they had touched and tasted and explored until she lost any coherent thought, he found the tight, aching bud between her thighs and she nearly rocketed off the bed.

He made a low, raw sound and, still kissing her, began to dance his fingers across her. Heat and desire and love wrapped her tightly in a cocoon of need, tighter and tighter until she couldn't breathe; her heart raced and her vision blurred. Finally he thrust a finger deep inside her and she cried out his name as the cocoon burst free and she soared.

When she fluttered back to earth, she found him watching her with those hot, hungry eyes. She pulled him to her for another kiss, one hand fisted in his hair, the other clutching him to her.

"I have to be inside," he groaned.

"Oh yes," she said fervently, then added a polite "please."

He laughed hoarsely. "I'm afraid I won't last very long," he said as he reached for one of the foil packets from the bedside table. "It's been so long for me."

She was breathless—nervous and still painfully aroused at once. "That's all right. We can take it slow the next time."

His eyes darkened at her inference that once wouldn't be enough, then he entered her with one powerful motion.

Though she tried to brace herself for it, Kate stiffened and swallowed her instinctive cry as she felt the resistance of her hymen break free with a deep, burning ache.

Hunter froze, his features stunned. "You're a frigging virgin!"

She had the completely insane urge to giggle at the oxymoron as the first pain began to ease. In the face of his fury, she decided it probably wouldn't be a good idea.

"Well, technically, not anymore."

He held himself rigid, unmoving for a few seconds, long enough for her to marvel at the novel, wonderful sensation. A man was inside her! Not just any man but Hunter Bradshaw. The man she had loved forever, long before she even could admit it to herself.

The ache all but forgotten, Kate wrapped her arms around

him and arched to angle him in deeper. Hunter's breathing was ragged, tortured, his neck corded with veins.

After a moment of holding himself absolutely still, he groaned. "I can't stop. I'm sorry."

"I don't want you to stop." She kissed him, her arms tight around him, as he surged deep inside her.

He drove into her no more than four or five times then with a hoarse cry he found release.

Kate held him close as long as he would let her, until his frenzied heartbeat slowed and his ragged breathing returned almost to normal.

After a moment, he slipped out of her arms and rose without a word, crossing to the bathroom to take care of the condom. She heard running water and then he returned to the bed with a warm washcloth for her to wash the streaky blood off her thighs.

"Why didn't you tell me?"

The quiet anger in his voice, so at odds with his considerate gesture, sliced at her composure but she took a deep breath and forced herself to meet his baffled, angry gaze. "Why? What difference does it make?"

"One hell of a lot! You know it does! I never would have let things go so far if I had known you had never been with a man before."

"Then I'm glad I didn't tell you. I wanted to make love to you, Hunter. I'm a grown woman and can make my own choices. Tonight, this was what I wanted."

"Why?"

He looked genuinely baffled at her behavior. She wanted to tell him she loved him, but she knew he wouldn't welcome the information.

Finally she shrugged, heat crawling up her cheekbones. "The moment seemed right," she said. She didn't want him to know the depth of her emotions—the last thing she wanted right now in addition to his anger was his pity—so she tried for a light, casual tone.

"You were here—a strong, warm, attractive man who appeared more than willing. Maybe I decided I was tired of wondering what all the fuss is about."

She regretted her glibness when a feral expression crossed his features. "I don't like being used, Kate. If you wanted a stud, you're looking in the wrong pasture."

Tears burned at his coldness but she knew she deserved it. "If that's all I wanted, why would I still be a virgin at twenty-six years old?"

He yanked on his jeans. "That's a question I would certainly like to know the answer to."

Kate drew the sheet around her, compelled to be honest about this, at least. "I've always thought I was too picky. Sex just never seemed a priority to me. I had my goals and I preferred to focus on them, not on anything that might be distracting. I never dated anyone who seemed worth the energy for all of this."

He continued watching her out of hooded eyes and she yearned for even a hint of softness in him.

"During one of her psych classes, Taylor told me I never date the same man more than a few times as a self-protective mechanism. She believed I use my experiences in childhood as a shield and a crutch. I don't let people too close because I look at everyone through the suspicious, wary eyes of a child who has been hurt one too many times.

"I don't know if either of those theories is true, mine or Taylor's," she went on. "I only know this was my choice, Hunter. One I'm glad I made, even if it will likely make things a little awkward between us for a while."

He made a disbelieving sound, as if to imply they had moved beyond awkward into excruciatingly uncomfortable.

"You should have told me," he said again. "At the least, I could have made things easier for you and not attacked you like some rutting beast."

"I'm sorry." The words seemed inadequate but she had nothing else to offer.

He studied her for a moment then he picked up his shirt. "I think it's best if I leave now," he said, his voice low, reserved. "Tomorrow will be a long day of driving to Miami."

She absorbed his rejection without even flinching. Determined to hide her hurt, she lifted her chin.

"I don't regret what happened between us, Hunter. Most of it was wonderful, until the last part there and even that was starting to feel good. I don't want you to regret it either."

He opened his mouth to say something, then closed it again and walked toward the door.

"Good night," he said brusquely, then he walked out into the hall. A moment later she heard the click of the door to the room next to hers, then all was silent.

Kate let out a long, pained breath. She meant what she'd said to him. She didn't regret making love to him, even with the empty bed and the empty space in her heart he had left behind.

She had a feeling years from now she would remember this wild-hair trip to Florida as one of those pivotal, life-changing events. Making love to Hunter would certainly qualify as pivotal in any woman's life, especially one who had loved him for years.

He might leave her heart bruised and her body aching. But every single moment had been worth the price of admission for the chance to be in his arms.

* * *

Kate had a feeling she was in for a long, uncomfortable day.

For one thing, a few restless hours of sleep did not put her at her best for traveling. She also had a whole range of sore muscles she hadn't expected from their extracurricular activities the night before.

To top it all off, her traveling companion could hardly force himself to look at her in the early morning sunlight.

"Ready?" Hunter asked, his voice terse and his eyes shielded behind Ray-Bans the color of espresso.

As I'll ever be, she thought, but gave him only a polite smile in response. What else could she do? Tell him that although she had been as close to him as two people could possibly be the night before, in the light of morning the idea of sitting next to him in a moving vehicle for eight hours seemed about as daunting as taking her boards with her eyes closed.

She decided not to risk saying anything, so she just climbed into the passenger seat of the SUV.

"I grabbed coffee and a bagel for you while I was walking Belle earlier," he said tersely once he had climbed in the driver's seat.

"Thanks," she murmured.

His only response was to shrug and reach for the radio. Soon the low voices of NPR's Morning Edition filled the vehicle, effectively squashing any conversation, had she been at all inclined to attempt any.

They rode for fifteen miles in a tense, awkward silence. She wondered if they would spend the whole day with this morning-after discomfort between them. Just when she was about to say something, her phone bleeped from her bag.

For the first time she could remember, she reached for it

eagerly, grateful for any interruption in the tension between her and Hunter.

"Hello?" she said after the second ring.

"Kate, this is Gage. Gage McKinnon."

Despite her grim mood, she couldn't contain a little smile at her brother's formal greeting—as if she knew any other strong, commanding men named Gage besides her oldest brother that he felt he had to qualify with his last name.

"Hello Gage. How are Allie and the girls?"

"Good. Great. Well, Anna picked up a bit of cold at the wedding so she's been home from preschool since Monday. Poor thing is miserable. Runny nose, sore throat, sniffles. The only thing that makes her feel better is me reading *Yertle the Turtle* to her. I've read it at least a hundred times in the last few days. Good thing her mother's a nurse because I don't know the first thing about comforting sick kids."

Her smile was a little broader by the time he wound down. She found it funny—and terribly sweet—that her taciturn brother could wax positively eloquent when it came to his stepdaughters. "Have you taken her to her pediatrician yet?"

"Yeah. Allie's got her all fixed up. Cough syrups, pain relievers, the works."

"Good. Give her a kiss for me."

"I'll do that." He cleared his throat. "That's not why I called, actually. Mom phoned me this morning and told me what you've been up to down there. I really wish you had talked to me first. I could have saved you three days of driving."

Her hands tightened on the phone as she absorbed his meaning. "You know where Brenda Golightly is?"

Gage didn't answer for a moment. When he did, she heard the regret in his voice. "Yeah. I know."

"Is the FBI investigating?"

"Twenty-three-year-old kidnapping cases are a fairly low priority to the bureau so Wyatt and I did a little digging on our own. We hired a P.I. and he tracked her down a few weeks ago. She's living in the Keys."

Her brothers had known where Brenda was all along. She stared out the windshield, her mind whirling. She didn't know much about the whole sibling dynamic but she was fairly certain keeping secrets like this one shouldn't be allowed.

"You and Wyatt both knew this and yet you never bothered to tell me?"

"We talked about it but we didn't think you wanted to know," Gage said warily. "If you'll remember, when I questioned you about the woman right after we received the DNA tests back confirming you were Charlotte, you said you didn't know where she was and you didn't care. You said you lost contact with her years ago and you didn't seem all that eager to find her again. I believe your exact words were *She can rot in hell as far as I care.*"

Kate winced, remembering her words. She had meant them at the time but that was before she had come to see that she would never be free of Brenda until she faced her one more time.

They knew where Brenda was. The implications of her brother's words started to seep in. She hadn't needed to drag Hunter into this at all. If she had only talked to Wyatt or Gage, she could have flown out and confronted Brenda on her own.

She had made a royal mess of this whole thing.

"Did you talk to her? Ask her how she ended up with me?"

Gage was quiet. "I didn't. Not personally," he finally

said. "I wanted to but I had some pending cases here I couldn't break away from for a trip right now. I had a friend of mine out of the Miami field office pay her a visit."

Kate waited for him to go on. When he said nothing, she fought the urge to grind her teeth. "And? What did she have to say?"

"Not much, Kate. I'm sorry. She wasn't in any condition to say much of anything."

"Let me guess. She was stoned."

"Not exactly." His voice gentled. "Brenda Golightly is in a Key West nursing home after a heroine overdose four years ago that left her with limited mental function. She wasn't sure of her own name, forget about remembering details of something that happened more than two decades ago."

The fist in her lap moved to her stomach as she tried to absorb one more blow. "Limited mental function. Does that mean she won't be prosecuted for what she did to me? To all of us?"

"I doubt it. After the report I got from my colleague, I don't see how Brenda Golightly could ever be found competent enough to stand trial, even if the Nevada statute of limitations on kidnappings hadn't run out years ago."

The woman had destroyed so many lives, had wrecked a good marriage, had taken an innocent child and thrust her into hell. Yet she would never pay for what she had done. The injustice of it was staggering.

"I'm sorry I didn't tell you," Gage said. "I see now I should have, no matter what you said about not wanting to ever see her again. But I never imagined for a moment you would suddenly decide to take off in the middle of the night to go after her."

"It was a last-minute thing," she said, still reeling. "I had some time off and it seemed like a good idea at the time."

"Well, you could always go to Disney World or something while you're down there. Or visit that foster couple who took such good care of you, the couple whose name you took."

Kate had a sudden powerful yearning to walk into the warm, cheerful kitchen of Tom and Maryanne Spencer, to smell Maryanne's African violets and see Tom's familiar, sturdy frame. She pushed it away and tried to focus on her brother.

"Good suggestions. Thanks. I'll have to see what Hunter thinks."

"Which brings us to the second reason for my call. What the hell were you thinking to head off across the country with a man like Bradshaw without telling anyone?"

Her hackles rose as she readied to defend the man who sat in the driver's seat, listening to every word as they drove past strip malls and warehouses. "I don't need a lecture from you, Gage."

"No, what you need is a hard kick in the seat. You scared Mom half to death when she couldn't reach you these last few days."

"I've already I told her I'm sorry for that. I'm not used to having anyone besides Taylor worrying about me and she and Wyatt are on their honeymoon. I didn't even think about calling anyone else about my plans."

"And the rest of it. Taking off with Bradshaw? Why is he involved?" Suspicion colored his voice. "Do the two of you have something going?"

An image from the night before danced across her mind, of mouths and bodies tangled together, and heat crept across her cheeks. "None of your business, Gage."

She knew she sounded rude but she had just about had it with big, handsome, overbearing men who thought they knew everything.

"Be careful, Kate," he said after a pause. "That's all I'm going to say. Be careful, for your sake and for mine."

"For yours?"

"Yeah. Prison can make any man—especially an innocent one—mean as a snake in a badger hole. I don't particularly want to have to try to whip Hunter Bradshaw's ass if he ends up hurting my baby sister."

To her surprise—and no doubt to Gage's—she laughed. "Thanks for your concern, but I can take care of myself."

"I know you can," he said gruffly. "You've done a good job of it so far. I just wanted to remind you that you've got a couple brothers on your side now. I might still be hobbling around with these bum legs but that doesn't mean I can't get the job done. And Wyatt is a whole lot tougher than he looks. Between the two of us, we ought to be able to take care of Bradshaw if he steps out of line."

"I'll keep that in mind. Thanks."

Chapter 11

A few moments later, Kate said goodbye to Gage then returned the phone to her bag. She leaned back against the leather of the seat, lost in thought.

Hunter waited as long as he could. "You planning to leave me in suspense all the way to Miami? What did he say?"

She opened one eye and peered at him. "He says he doesn't want to beat you up if you hurt his baby sister but he will. And Wyatt will help. That's what big brothers are for, apparently—a side benefit I hadn't fully appreciated when the McKinnons found me."

"Good to know. Did he have anything else to say?"

"Oh, not really."

She dropped the light tone and opened both eyes. In them he saw a mix of emotions—regret and apology and no small amount of embarrassment. "Only that I've dragged you and Belle three thousand miles on a wild goose chase."

"Oh?"

"I should have called him first. I'm so stupid. It never even occurred to me to start with Gage. I'm so used to doing everything on my own that I have to keep reminding myself I even have brothers, one of whom works for the FBI. Apparently he and Wyatt have known for a few weeks now that Brenda Golightly is in a nursing home in Key West. An OD a few years ago left her brain-damaged."

She said the last in a flat tone at odds to the tumult in her eyes.

Brain-damaged. Hunter didn't miss the implications. No punishment, no vengeance, no answers.

"I'm sorry, Kate."

She gazed out the windshield, her color high. "You must think I'm such a fool. I can't believe we've come this far for nothing."

"I don't think you're a fool. I think you're a victim of a terrible crime who wanted to find answers. Who *deserved* to find answers. What could possibly be foolish about that?"

"Well, it looks like I'll never find them now. The whys and the hows are probably locked away somewhere in Brenda Golightly's drug-ravaged mind."

He hated seeing her features haunted by pain.

"I suppose we should just turn around and start heading back to Salt Lake City," she went on. "There's no reason to drag this out any further."

A few hours earlier when he had been sitting awake in that damn hotel room after a sleepless night castigating himself and her, he might have agreed with her that they should just cut their losses and go home.

Faced with her pain, he had a difficult time remembering the anger that had prowled through him like a caged animal since making love with her the night before.

He hadn't been mad at her. Not really, though he supposed she no doubt believed otherwise after the abrupt, rude way he left her.

Wham, bam, thank you ma'am.

While he still believed she should have told him she had never been with a man, most of his anger was self-directed. He had given into his overwhelming need without giving any thought to the consequences. For three long days he had fought his attraction for her and then in an instant all his hard work, every bit of control and self-denial, had been for nothing.

None of that seemed important suddenly. Not with Kate in the seat next to him, looking like she had just been kicked in the teeth. The need to comfort her, to ease that pain in her eyes, was stronger than any lingering anger.

"We're not turning around."

She blinked. "We're not?"

"No. We can't just give up. We're this close, Kate. We can make it to Key West in time to watch the sunset."

"To what end? There's no point in dragging this out. Don't you get it? Brenda can't tell us anything. Gage sent one of his FBI colleagues to talk to her and from the sound of it she was barely coherent."

"She might not have said much to an FBI agent but that doesn't necessarily follow that she won't have anything to say to you. I've seen brain injuries before and I know how capricious they can be. You should know that, Dr. Spencer. Who knows, you could have better luck getting through than a stranger."

They traveled a full mile before she spoke again. "She might not even know who I am. What if she doesn't say anything more to me than she did to Gage's colleague?"

"Then she doesn't. You may never find the answers you

want. I guess you'll have to be ready for that eventuality. But at least it won't be for lack of trying on our part."

She still looked unconvinced, her hands fisted together on her lap.

"Besides, I've never been to Key West," Hunter went on, undeterred by her silence. "Maybe I can take Taylor home a conch shell for Christmas."

"Why?"

"Well, I'd like to take her a palm tree but I don't think it will fit in the cargo area."

She frowned. "No, why do you insist on dragging this out? After last night, I would think you should be more than ready to turn back."

His jaw hardened at her reference to the evening before. "The job's not done. I offered to help you and I'll see it through."

"Don't you think you're carrying this damsel-in-distress thing a little far?"

Maybe. If he were smart, he would be doing all he could to spend as little time as possible with a woman who left him aching and confused. He would have seen the wisdom of cutting their trip as short as possible, returning to Salt Lake City and going their separate ways.

A sane man—or at least a smart one—certainly wouldn't be coming up with transparent excuses to spend as much time as possible with a woman he knew he couldn't have.

"We've come this far, Kate. Let's see it through."

She looked undecided for a moment, then nodded tightly.

She wasn't sure how he did it, but Hunter was able miraculously to find deluxe lodging in Key West that welcomed pets, after only a few phone calls. The two tiny matching cottages were set in a lush tropical garden overlooking the Gulf of Mexico. Both painted a pale, cheerful pink, they looked like the perfect spot for a breezy, relaxing beach vacation.

Too bad she wasn't here to relax.

Under other circumstances she would have found it restful swinging in the hammock on the small wood porch while palm fronds rustled and swayed overhead and the ocean licked the sand twenty yards away.

If not for the low, steady thrum of anger—the deep, restlessness that seemed to have increased the closer they drove to this isolated paradise—she would have loved this.

She had come to the Keys once with Tom and Maryanne. They had stayed not far from here, she remembered.

The trip had been a panacea of sorts—a consolation prize—to offset their deep disappointment after Brenda once more had refused to relinquish her parental rights so Kate could be officially adopted by the Spencers.

Her entire adolescence had been one long tug-of-war with Brenda. With the Spencers, Kate had finally found a place where she could be content, could belong. Yet Brenda had refused time and again to let them make their foster arrangement permanent.

Kate had been fourteen that long-ago trip to the Keys, trying desperately to figure out why Brenda didn't want her but didn't seem to want anyone else to have her either.

She and Tom and Maryanne had gone through the motions of enjoying themselves on that trip, she remembered now. They had walked and shopped along Duval Street and the rest of Old Town, had snorkeled, had even gone out deep-sea fishing where Tom had caught a swordfish that still hung in his office in St. Petersburg.

But through it all, a dark, greasy cloud had hung over them, a shadow they couldn't shake. Brenda, with her lies and her manipulations and her dogged determination that Kate remain legally hers.

It wasn't as if Brenda had wanted to play a huge part in her life in those eleven years after Kate had been removed from her custody until she'd reached eighteen and could legally change her name.

Brenda had come only occasionally for the court-approved visit, just often enough that Kate couldn't be considered abandoned and therefore become eligible for adoption.

She had come to dread those brief, uncomfortable encounters that always left her angry and depressed for weeks.

The real hell of it was that she hadn't hated Brenda. Not at first, anyway. That had come later, as she had moved further into her teens.

No, for most of her childhood before she had landed with the Spencers, Kate had loved the woman she thought was her mother—loved her with single-minded, childlike affection and desperately wanted her approval, waiting for the day when Brenda would claim her and they could be together again.

For all Brenda's selfishness, her addictions, her men, she had been the only constant in Kate's life as she was shuttled from home to home, the one thing she had to hold onto for as far back as she could remember.

The troubled child she had been was frightened of Brenda—of the chaos and tumult of their life—but she had loved her.

Sitting on the porch of this cheerful little cottage by the sea, Kate felt an echo of that love and couldn't stop her heavy sigh. How could she have loved a woman who treated her with such callous indifference? Why hadn't she *known* somehow that their whole relationship was a fraud?

Since finding out about her past, she had scoured the deep recesses of her memory bank trying for even one instance when she might have suspected Brenda wasn't really her mother. She could come up with nothing. She had only a vague, very early memory—not even a memory, really, more just a hazy impression—of a time when her life had been happy, safe.

Charlotte McKinnon might have been happy in her safe, comfortable world but poor little Katie Golightly had never enjoyed that luxury.

She sighed again, hating this self-pity, just as Hunter walked up the steps to the porch with the suitcase he had insisted on carrying up from the Jeep for her.

He set it down inside the cottage, then rejoined her on the porch, leaning against a pillar.

"Want to grab a bite to eat before we head over to the nursing home?" he asked.

She turned to face him, for the first time noting how the hard lines around his mouth seemed to have eased a little. In the slanted sunlight filtering through the lush growth in bright patches, his features seemed less harsh than they had four days earlier.

He was gorgeous, so beautifully male that her stomach did a long, slow roll.

"I'm not very hungry."

"No problem. We can get something a little later, after we talk to Brenda."

The dread that had ridden with her all afternoon seemed to wash over her again, drenching her like a sudden tropical rain.

She exhaled slowly. "I…Hunter, would you mind if we waited until the morning to go to the nursing home?"

He raised an eyebrow. "Why? We're here now. You've come three thousand miles for answers."

"Answers we both know I'm not likely to ever find now."

"You certainly won't find them if you refuse to even go talk to the woman."

"I will talk to her," she insisted. "But not yet. I know you probably think I'm crazy or the world's biggest coward but I…I just can't yet. I need to work up to it. Can we wait until morning?"

He studied her. "You're not crazy."

"Well, I seem to be doing a pretty good imitation of it then. I *feel* crazy. Restless and angry. Itchy inside my own skin. I want to scream and shout and throw chairs around one minute and curl up into a ball and cry my eyes out the next."

"Sounds pretty normal to me."

She laughed a little at his dry tone. "I guess that proves we're both a little wacky."

"That's certainly a possibility."

Kate had a sudden vivid memory of the wild heat they'd generated between them the night before and had to take a deep breath to calm her suddenly racing heart.

"Crazy or not," she said when she could think again, "I can't face Brenda yet. I just can't, Hunter. I need a little more time."

Hunter studied her in the dappled tropical light. She looked fragile and tired, her eyes huge in her pale face. With each mile they drove closer to Key West he had seen the finely wrought tension on her features, her body posture. By the time he'd found these cottages, she was so tightly strung it was a wonder she didn't vibrate.

He couldn't blame her for being nervous about meeting the woman who had caused her such pain. He still hadn't been able to bring himself to see Martin James since his release. His former defense attorney was in the county jail awaiting sentencing after pleading guilty to a host of charges, including the capital-murder charges he had ostensibly been defending Hunter on, though Martin had done everything possible to make sure his client would pay for his own crimes.

Martin was expected to receive the same sentence he had done his best behind the scenes to make sure Hunter had received—death by lethal injection.

Hunter doubted he would ever have the strength of will to face Martin as Kate was facing her demons. A least not without wanting to be the one shoving in that needle—not just because Martin had framed him but for Dru and her dying mother and her unborn baby. And because Martin had been willing to kill Taylor to keep his deadly secrets.

He wouldn't even go see Martin, so how could he blame Kate for needing a little time to prepare herself before confronting her pain?

"Okay. This is your show," he said. "There's no reason we can't go in the morning."

Her smile flashed like a heron taking flight. "Thank you."

That smile entranced him and he wanted nothing more in that moment than to stand in the warm sunlight and soak it in.

Well, okay, he did want something more. He wanted to capture that smile with his mouth, to absorb her sighs and her pain into him.

Hunger gnawed at him, making a mockery of any hope he might have been foolish enough to entertain that the night before might have worked her out of his system.

He couldn't kiss her and he couldn't afford a repeat of the night before. The very fact of her inexperience had driven that home forcefully through the long night and their drive south across Florida.

Kate was a relationship kind of woman with a capital *R*. She obviously wasn't interested in casual sex or she wouldn't have still been a virgin, and he wasn't capable of anything else right now.

He was empty inside. No, not completely empty. There seemed to be room for his hate and anger—and even some irrational shame—over what had happened to him. But anything good and decent had died during those grim days and miserable nights of his incarceration.

He would hurt her. He didn't want to but he knew himself well enough to know it was inevitable. He couldn't do it to her—she was coping with enough pain right now.

He shoved his hands in his pockets to keep from reaching for her, good intentions be damned. "I think I'll take Belle for a run on the beach. We can both use it after four days on the road."

She looked as if she would like to go along but right now he needed distance from her to rebuild his self-control, so he refrained from issuing an invitation.

"I'll be done in an hour or so. If you're hungry by then, we can wander out and see what we can find to eat."

He'd heard the nightlife on Key West was wild and woolly. He wasn't much of a drinker but maybe if he got good and smashed he might be able to forget the night before and the healing peace he had known so briefly in her arms.

He was still feeling vaguely unsettled after he'd changed into a T-shirt and the one pair of jogging shorts he'd brought along.

Belle was beside herself with joy, anticipating exactly what was coming. She panted with glee and raced circles around him as they headed out toward the water.

They had made good time from Jacksonville that day. Hunter had predicted they would be in Key West by sunset and, sure enough, the sun was just beginning its slow slide into the sea as he set a hard pace for himself through the hard-packed sand close to the waves.

Lord, he loved this. Euphoria churned through his veins with every step, every thud of his jogging shoes in the sand.

Of all the things he had missed during his three years of incarceration, the freedom to take off and run whenever the mood hit him had been up there close to the top of his list. Exercise had certainly been encouraged for inmates. Corrections officers figured it worked off aggression better expended in sweat and exertion than on each other. But Hunter found little satisfaction running around a prison-yard track like a rat in a cage.

He did it anyway, along with weight lifting to keep his body in shape. But every time he would run inside those razor wire–tipped walls, he would dream of a moment like this, of stretching his legs as far as they would go and heading off into the sunset.

The ocean was a new twist. Usually his prison fantasies involved taking off into the mountains surrounding his home in Little Cottonwood Canyon, the sharp tang of sage surrounding him and the clear, high air burning his lungs while Belle chased after ground squirrels and pikas.

This was a heaven he wouldn't even have let himself dream about two months ago—water lapping at the sand, the warm sea breeze kissing his skin, the sun slipping toward the Gulf of Mexico in a fiery show of orange and purple.

Hunter enjoyed the sunset on the go, unwilling to stop even for something so spectacular, not with the endorphin high pumping through his system.

With Belle chasing the waves excitedly and shorebirds crying overhead, it was a moment of pure, stunning joy. The euphoria almost made up for his four days on the road, of trying—and obviously failing spectacularly—to keep his hands off Kate.

He ran for a long time, until his lungs ached and the sun dipped into the water. As he headed back up the beach toward their rented cottages, his mind traveled of its own will to the woman who waited there.

Small and lovely and vulnerable, she made a dangerous package, one he found entirely too appealing. He just had to do his best to resist her, no matter what it took.

His resolve was tested unexpectedly about a quarter mile from their lodging. The sun was now only a rim above the waves but he still had enough light to see a solitary figure on the beach staring out to sea, arms wrapped around her knees.

He knew instantly it was Kate.

Even if he hadn't recognized the sunlit warmth of her hair or that slender, elegant stretch of neck, he would have known it was her by Belle's joyful reaction. The dog raced to her side and leaped and writhed to see her as if they had been separated for months and hadn't just spent the last three days in almost constant company.

Kate hugged Belle to her and even from a dozen yards away he could hear her low laughter. It slid around and through him like a thin, silvery ribbon.

He stopped there in the sand, his muscles twitching and his heart still pounding from the run.

Still sitting in the sand, she swiveled a little to face him, a small smile of welcome on her face.

Coming home. That's what he felt like when he saw her, like some part of him that had been adrift for too long at last had a place to rest.

He stared at her as a stunning realization hit him with the jolt of a thousand watts of electricity.

He was in love with her.

These last few days on this trip—hell, for the whole five years he had known her—he had done his best to convince himself this *thing* between them was only physical attraction. Pheromone to pheromone, yin to yang.

Standing here with the tropical breeze cooling the sweat on his body and the sea a soft wash of colors behind him, he forced himself finally to face the truth he had been running from.

They shared an attraction, certainly. A constant, insidious heat that made him aware of her every sigh, her every breath.

But he could no longer deny the truth. This was far more than a mere physical attraction. He was in love with Kate Spencer, of the healer's spirit and the troubled past and the haunted eyes.

He loved her laughter and he loved her courage and he loved the way she gathered stray chicks around her like a lonely mother hen.

The realization horrified him. For a long moment, he could do nothing but stand there in the sand trying to catch his breath with his solar plexus tight and quivering as if he'd just taken a hard hit with one of those vicious billy clubs a couple of the guards at the Point of the Mountain took great delight in wielding against someone who had once been one of their own.

"How was your run?" she asked.

He cleared his throat, hoping she would attribute his sudden breathlessness to the exercise.

"Good. It's a beautiful place for a workout."

She lifted her face to the warm air. "I'd forgotten how

much I love the sea," she said with a soft smile. "Since I moved to Utah I've come to love the wildness—the primitive strength—of the Rockies. But the ocean feeds my soul."

He should leave, he thought with an edge of desperation. Right now, run as fast as he could away from her. Instead, he found himself moving closer. He knew it was foolish but still he found himself sitting beside her in the sand, though he maintained what he hoped was a safe distance between them.

"Why did you leave Florida? I'm sure you could have gone somewhere closer to med school. What took you to the University of Utah?"

Her brow furrowed as she considered his question. "I don't know that I have a firm answer to that. Not one that makes any sense, anyway. I was accepted to three different medical schools—Vanderbilt, Tulane and the University of Utah. I was really close to going to Vanderbilt but somehow the mountains called to me. Somewhere deep in my soul were memories of aspens and pines and blue sky. I used to think it was some lingering remnant of a previous life."

Her small laugh contained little humor. "I guess it was. That first time I went back to Liberty with Gage and Wyatt, they drove me to Lynn's house, on my grandfather's ranch where we all lived for the first three years of my life. I can remember looking up at the green-and-gray mountains surrounding the ranch and feeling this deep connection, this missing piece of my life clicking back into place."

She was quiet as the first stars started peeking out of the twilight sky. "I didn't know why until this last month or so but I suppose I left Florida looking for that missing piece of myself. For my family."

"And you found them."

"Right, even though technically, they found me. Anyway,

Utah is home now and was before the McKinnons ever found me but a part of my soul will always hunger for the ocean. I suppose this is one of those painful times I have to give up one thing I love in order to get something else I love."

"The ocean will always be here waiting whenever you come back."

She gave a little laugh. "You're right. I really don't have to choose, do I?"

"Not right now anyway. Right now you can just enjoy it."

They sat for several moments in silence, Belle flopped onto the sand beside them, while the waves lapped at the shore and the stars continued to pop out like silver sequins.

"I'm sorry I disturbed your run," she said after a moment.

"We were heading back anyway. I haven't quite got my running legs back."

Her gaze shifted to his legs and he was unnerved to see color rise on her cheeks. The brief moment of peace suddenly seemed charged with tension, awareness.

Hunter cleared his throat. He had to get out of here before he did something stupid.

He rose, shaking sand off. "I, uh, need to shower and then we can find somewhere to eat if you're up for it." Somewhere crowded and noisy and raucous where he wouldn't have to be alone with her.

She nodded, her color still high. "Okay."

"You want to stay here a little longer?"

"No. I think I'm ready to go back."

He helped her to her feet but quickly released her hand as they walked up the deep white sand toward their cottages. He couldn't risk prolonged physical contact right now, not with this thick emotion swirling through him.

He needed space and distance from her. Too bad he

couldn't swim out to some isolated offshore cay and stay there for a week or two, until she returned to Utah and her residency.

Chapter 12

How did a woman with very little experience seduce the man she loved?

Kate blew out a breath, for once wishing she'd taken more time away from medical textbooks in the last few years to gain a little practical knowledge.

She knew how to discourage a man, to slip away from wandering hands and to gently divert a man's attention until he didn't even realize he had been brushed off.

That she could do in her sleep. The opposite—letting a man know she wanted more—was a little harder to figure out. How did she do it without coming across as easy or desperate or both?

The trouble was, she only had about fifteen minutes to figure it out before Hunter finished showering and changing from his jogging clothes. Fifteen minutes to turn herself from bland to bombshell.

It was a daunting prospect.

Kate stood in her cheerful rented cottage, a ceiling fan spinning lazily overhead as she studied the pitiful offerings from her suitcase spread out across her tropical bedspread.

She might have had a fighting chance if she had brought along something slinky and sultry, an outfit sure to turn her petite, almost boyish figure into something that cried out *ba-da-bing*.

Okay, that would take more than a sexy outfit to accomplish. Still, it would be nice to have something to work with here.

When she had packed in those early morning hours after the wedding—what seemed a lifetime ago—she had opted for travel casual, clothes picked more for comfort than for their sex appeal.

The only thing she'd brought along that was even remotely interesting was the simple, no-frills black dress she'd picked up before her Guatemala trip, mostly because it was guaranteed not to wrinkle.

With a snap of her wrists she shook it, relieved when she found the short-sleeved tunic dress lived up to its hype and was ready for a night on the town. At least she had the foresight to include a pair of flat black sandals to go with it— wouldn't she have looked lovely with her little black dress and high-tops?—but she was afraid she still looked like some kind of granola lover.

The only thing she had for accessories was a handmade Mayan jade *mariposa* necklace-and-earring set she'd bought at a village market in Guatemala. No problem. At least it would match the butterflies in her stomach.

Kate blew out a breath, slipped into the dress and went to work on her hair and makeup, something she rarely fussed with. Anticipation curled through her as she piled her hair onto her head, wishing she had time for something a little more elegant, then quickly applied eye shadow, mascara and the sexiest shade of lipstick she owned. Her color was high enough she decided she didn't need blush.

Sultry. That's what she was going for here. Maybe Hunter would be swept away by the hot, uninhibited tropical nights. She could always dream, couldn't she?

One would hope that after four days in his constant company, she could read the man a little better but he was still a mystery, a study in contrasts. There had been that odd, jittery moment on the beach earlier when he had gazed at her with an intense light in his midnight eyes that left her shaky and breathless.

But then he barely touched her. She hadn't missed how quickly he had released her hand after helping her from the sand. That hadn't been the only example. All day, he'd gone out of his way to avoid even the most accidental of touches.

Maybe the reason for his distance was something other than revulsion. She thought of the expression in those eyes and pressed a hand to her stomach through the black cotton at the nerves jumping there.

She had to believe Hunter wasn't completely unaffected by her. He had certainly been interested enough the night before, even when she had been teary and emotional.

She was just finishing up when a knock sounded at the door. Blotting her lipstick, Kate took time for one quick look in the mirror. Not bad for travel chic.

Ready or not, Hunter Bradshaw.

"Just a minute," she called, then slipped into the sandals and hurried to the door.

When she opened the door, the butterflies in her stomach turned into stampeding rhinos. He stood on the other side wearing khakis and a navy-blue golf shirt, his wet hair gleaming silvery black in the porch light. He smelled divine, that sexy, cedary male aftershave that transported her instantly to the night before, trailing kisses up his neck.

For just a moment, she thought his eyes turned hot and hungry as he looked at her in her little black travel dress, but he blinked and the moment was gone.

She tried to smile a greeting but was fairly certain her facial muscles had suddenly gone Botox-numb on her, along with everything else.

"Where's Belle?" It was the only thought her brain could grab hold of.

"Enjoying a minute to herself, I think. She was sound asleep in her crate when I left."

She continued to stand there like an idiot and only realized it when he cleared his throat. "Are you ready?" he asked.

Oh yes, she wanted to say but she swallowed the fervent declaration. "I think so," she said instead. "Oh wait. I forgot."

Kate grabbed the jade butterfly necklace and earrings off the dresser. To her dismay, her hands that could suture a gaping wound with tiny, delicate stitches fumbled with something as simple as inserting the earrings in her ears, but she finally managed it.

She picked up the necklace and reached her arms behind her neck to fasten it, then she happened to glance at Hunter. She found him staring at her, his eyes slightly unfocused and his respiration rate most definitely accelerated.

Hmmm. Maybe this whole seduction business wasn't as tough as she feared. She took a deep breath and decided to try the only thing she could come up with at short notice.

"I can't quite work the clasp," she murmured after a moment. "Would you mind helping me?"

He froze, a trapped look in his eyes, then she saw his throat work. "I'm not very good with jewelry thingies. You look fine without the necklace."

"I'd really like to wear it, though."

After a few heartbeats, the trapped look gave way to resignation. He took the necklace from her and moved behind her. She obliged by tipping her head forward, pulling the stray tendrils of hair that always managed to slip from her updo out of the way.

Just who was seducing whom here? Kate wondered as Hunter went to work on the necklace. She was painfully aware of him, of his just-showered scent and his crisp, clean clothes and his fingers warm and strong against her skin.

A shiver slid down her spine at his touch and she closed her eyes and leaned her head back until it rested against his shoulder.

His fingers at her nape stilled and she could feel the quick rise and fall of his chest. "What are you doing, Kate?" he asked, his voice low.

Hot color soaked her cheeks. She couldn't come up with anything but the truth, so she straightened and turned to face him. "I was hoping to seduce you, but I'm obviously not very good at it."

His short laugh was raw, unamused. "I wouldn't say that."

That sounded promising. "No?"

"If you leaned any closer, you would find out exactly how you affect me."

Her gaze locked with his. "Is that an invitation?"

A muscle flexed in his jaw. "Dammit, Kate. This isn't a good idea."

"Why not?"

He groaned. "A hundred reasons. If I were a smart man

I would have turned around the moment I walked in the door and found you in that dress. I have no self-control where you're concerned."

"Good," she murmured, then stepped forward again, her arms entwined around his neck as she kissed him.

He stayed unmoving for perhaps ten seconds, then he groaned and dragged her against him.

He must have shaved again after his shower. That sexy dark shadow she had seen him grow by evening over the last few days was gone and his skin smelled of that delicious aftershave.

His kiss was edged by the same wild desperation of the night before. This time it didn't unnerve her, it only fueled her own desire.

"Make love to me again Hunter. Please."

He closed his eyes as if praying for strength. When he opened them, they were dark, aroused. "All day I've tried to convince myself what a mistake that would be, no matter how much I might want it."

She pressed her mouth to his carotid artery, to the pulse she could see pumping just below the skin. "Did it work?"

"What do you think? I'm not very persuasive, I guess. Right now making love to you seems like the best idea in the world."

"I'm glad we see eye to eye," she murmured and kissed him again.

"I don't want to hurt you, Kate."

He wasn't talking about the kind of fleeting physical pain she had experienced the night before. She sensed it, could almost feel a phantom spasm from the impending heartache.

"You won't," she lied, lifting her chin. "I can take care of myself."

He didn't look convinced so she kissed him again, pouring all the emotions she couldn't say into her kiss, her touch.

The dress she had selected with such care quickly ended up piled on the floor. Busy helping him out of his clothes, Kate left it there, grateful for the wonders of wrinkle-free cloth.

As inevitable as the tide, they came together, unspoken emotions simmering below the surface. This time there was no anger, no fear, only this wild, edgy heat.

"Are you still sore?" Hunter asked just before he entered her.

Kate thought about denying it but honesty compelled her to nod. "Maybe a little. Don't worry about it, though."

She should have known he would. The kind of man who rode his silver SUV to the rescue of any damsel in distress who needed him would die before he hurt his woman.

Not his woman, she reminded herself. His lover. For now, that would have to be enough.

After a moment's consideration, Hunter rolled onto his back, pulling her atop him. Kate gasped as he guided her onto his arousal.

"You have a little better control this way." His voice was raspy, deep. "If anything hurts, you can stop."

Nice theory, but she knew she couldn't have stopped even if a hurricane suddenly blew across the Key.

Kate twisted her fingers around his, setting an erotically slow pace. With each deep thrust inside her, she had to clamp down on the words of love fluttering in her throat like trapped birds.

Heat and love and desire braided through her, tighter and tighter, binding her to this strong, beautiful man with the shadows in his eyes.

At last, just when she was sure she couldn't endure another moment, he reached a finger to the junction of their bodies and touched her. With a wild cry, she soared free. He watched her, his eyes hot and dark, then he gripped her fingers again and with one more powerful surge, joined her.

Much later, when every muscle burned with a pleasant exhaustion, she lay nestled in the crook of his shoulder, her arm spread across the hard muscles of chest.

"We didn't get dinner."

She laughed at the woeful note in his voice and raised up a little so she could see his face better.

"If not for the last hour or so I would have said some smart remark about food being the only thing you think about."

To her shock, he grinned. Hunter Bradshaw actually grinned, a slow, sexy smile that made her just about forget her name. As she looked at him sprawled there in the bed of her rented cottage, she felt as if she'd just been handed the world.

"I think about plenty of things. Food. Sex. Food. Sex. I'm a man of many interests."

Oh, she wanted to hold on tight and never let this lighthearted man go. If she had helped him, even a little, to allow some goodness back into his life she thought it would almost be worth the heartache she knew waited for her back in Utah.

"How about pizza?" she suggested. "I'm sure Ruben and Violet could suggest a decent place that delivers."

He agreed and called the small resort's owners at the front office. They recommended a place not far from their lodging that delivered delicious pizza. After some debate, they decided to be adventurous and ordered something billed as a Caribbean pie, with grilled chicken, pineapples and peppers on a plum sauce instead of the traditional tomato.

"We have half an hour before they deliver," Hunter said after he hung up.

She curled a hand across that hard chest, loving the way his pulse skipped a little at her touch. "Time management is a very important skill for medical residents. You'd be surprised what I can accomplish in half an hour."

He lifted her fist to his mouth and pressed a kiss to her knuckles. "Somehow I don't think anything you do could surprise me, Dr. Spencer."

"There's always a first time," she said with a sly smile, then proceeded to demonstrate.

He couldn't get enough of her.

After the pizza arrived and was quickly consumed, they took a shower together and made love again, this time slow and easy, with a tenderness that terrified him as much as it seduced him.

He would have been happy to stay there all night—hell, if he died in Kate's bed, he wasn't sure he would mind—but Belle had been stuck in her crate all evening.

Kate insisted on going with him and said she was eager to see Key West again, so while he retrieved Belle from his own room, Kate once more put on that sexy short black dress.

She was waiting for him on the porch of her cottage when he brought the dog out on her leash.

Even at 11:00 p.m. on a Wednesday night, the Key West nightlife was jumping. Live music blared from a half-dozen bars as they made their slow way down Duval Street, and the area was thronged with tourists.

It reminded him of a law-enforcement conference he'd attended in New Orleans just after he'd earned his gold shield. A couple of veteran detectives had dragged him down to the French Quarter with them and the rowdy party mood there had been the same.

This kind of crowd made the short hairs on the back of a cop's neck stand up. It could turn unpredictable in an instant.

He found himself scanning the crowd for any lawbreakers. When he realized it, he ordered himself to cut it out. He wasn't a cop anymore. He wasn't *anything,* just an ex-con in love with a woman who deserved far better than him.

The familiar restless dark mood crept up to the edge of his psyche. Hunter knew it was there, just waiting to take over, but he pushed it away. Tonight he wasn't going to give in. Tonight he had a beautiful woman on his arm, they were in a tropical paradise, and he was a free man. He intended to do his best to enjoy every minute of it.

"I'm in the mood for some key lime pie," he said suddenly. "What do you think?"

She smiled. "Sounds great."

They found a sidewalk café where Belle could rest at their feet and they could enjoy the sights and sounds of the warm night.

After they placed their order for pie, he told Kate of that convention in New Orleans when he'd been a rookie detective and how pathetically eager he had been to return to the clear, sweet mountain air of Utah when it was over.

She told him of her culture shock after moving to Utah from St. Petersburg but how she had learned to embrace some of the state idiosyncrasies.

Throughout their conversation, he was aware of her, of the way she tucked a stray tendril of honey-blond hair behind her ears, how she fingered that jade butterfly in the hollow of her neck, the absent way she sometimes reached down to pet Belle.

He was crazy about her. Everything she did.

He wanted this moment to stretch on forever.

He was so busy watching Kate, he almost missed a couple of drunks across the street when they staggered out of a bar, drinks in hand. He only noticed them when one started hassling a couple of women walking by.

"Come on, baby. Lemme buy you a drink," one said, loud enough to draw more than just Hunter's attention.

They looked like college boys who hadn't yet learned their limits, he thought. It was months too early for spring break but maybe they decided spending the holidays drunk in Key West would be a hell of a lot more fun than stringing popcorn back home with Mom and Dad.

The women quickly walked past but the frat boys were just warming up. Hunter watched as they accosted two or three more groups of women. He was just about to get up and tactfully urge them along when he saw a middle-aged man walking with what looked like his wife and teenage daughter.

The college boys said something to the daughter that had the man bristling. He could see by the alarming red of the father's face that whatever the drunks said had been offensive.

With a growing sense of inevitability, he watched the confrontation escalate and a moment later, the older man poked one of the boys in the chest with his finger.

· Hunter half rose, then forced himself to sit down again. Not his problem. He wasn't a cop anymore and he wasn't responsible for policing the whole damn world.

The frat boy apparently didn't like being dressed down by this stranger anymore than he probably did from his own father. When the man continued to get into his face, he cold-cocked him with a hard right.

The women screamed as the older man went down, clutching his nose, now spurting red.

In an instant, Hunter swore, handed Belle's leash to Kate and ordered her to stay put.

He managed to reach the trio before the outraged father came up swinging. As much as he understood and applauded the man's need to defend his women, these two cocky little bastards would beat the crap out of a pasty-white tourist like him.

"Bring it on, dude. Let's see what you got." The slightly bleary-eyed college kid stood over the tourist, baiting him to defend himself.

Hunter moved in between the two before the tourist could stagger to his feet.

"That's enough," he said in his best prison-yard tough voice. "Let's all just cool off now."

Frat Boy Number One blinked at him as if Hunter had just beamed in from the planet Zorcon. "Who'r'you?" he slurred.

Hunter ignored the question and turned to the tourist, whose wife and daughter fluttered around him like a couple of quail protecting their nest.

"Sir, are you all right?"

"Little bugger broke my nose."

Hunter was remarkably unsurprised when Kate disobeyed his order to stay out of harm's way and pushed her way through the crowd that had begun to gather. She handed Belle's leash to a bystander and knelt at the man's side. "Let me take a look at it. I'm a doctor."

Drunk far past the point of reason or discretion, Frat Boy Number Two leered at Kate kneeling there in her sexy little black dress and grabbed at his crotch. "Hey doc, I got something right here that hurts. Want to kiss it better?"

Hunter let out a disgruntled sigh, wondering why trouble seemed to follow them around like a greasy dark cloud, then he stepped forward, grabbed the punk by his shirtfront and shoved him into the other boy. Both of them went sprawling against the wall, amid widespread applause from the crowd.

The first kid came up swinging and managed to sneak an uppercut into Hunter's gut but the punch was so wimpy he barely felt it. He dodged the next one and returned it with a hard blow that knocked the college boy to the ground. He groaned but didn't get back up.

The other kid—the one with the dirty mouth—started to scurry away but his retreat was stopped by a couple of uniform cops on bicycles who had been drawn by the commotion.

"Why are we always in the wrong place at the wrong time?" Hunter muttered twenty minutes later when they finally returned to the café and their uneaten pie after giving their statements to the bike cops. The cops had hassled him a little about shoving the frat boys, but after they heard from various witnesses that Dumb and Dumber had started the altercation and had repeatedly accosted various women, they backed off.

The two college boys were on their way to face drunk-and-disorderly charges and the tourist's injuries had been treated at the scene.

"I think we're always in the right place at exactly the right time," Kate said.

She hadn't stopped looking at him with that soft light in her eyes, as if he were some kind of hero or something. He wanted to tell her to cut it out, that they were just a couple of drunk kids and he hadn't done anything, but he would rather just see the whole thing dropped.

She picked up his hand where his fist had been scraped a little on the kid's tooth in the altercation. "We'd better get this cleaned up. We should have had the paramedics look at it when they were helping Mr. Coletti. We can go back to the resort for my bag or I can see if the restaurant has a first-aid kit."

"It's fine, doc. Just a couple of scraped knuckles."

"Humor me, okay? Human bite wounds can be nasty."

She grabbed their waiter on his next go-round. A few moments later he brought a first-aid kit. Hunter stoically endured her fussing over him, washing off his knuckles and bandaging the worst scrape.

Not for all the world would he admit he secretly enjoyed her nurturing. It had been so long since he'd had this kind of softness and caring in his life, and he found himself soaking it up.

"There you go," she said, rubbing a finger over one of his uninjured knuckles. "Good as new."

Now if she could only do the same to his heart, but he was afraid it would never be the same.

They finished their remaining few bites of pie, then left a hefty tip for the waiter who had held their table for them during the street scene.

"Have you given any more thought to what you're going to do when we return to Utah?" Kate asked as they walked up the beach toward their lodging.

Besides try to live in a dull, colorless world without her? He hadn't managed to move beyond that. He shook his head. "Some. I haven't figured anything out yet."

"I think you should go back to being a cop."

"Don't you think I've been punished enough?"

She made a face at him. "It's not a punishment. It was a joy for you. I know it was."

He gazed at the moonlight shimmering on the water. "Maybe three years ago. That was a different lifetime ago. I was a different person."

"I saw you tonight as you handled those drunks. You were perfect—not vicious, just firm. Exactly what a good cop does."

"A good cop doesn't punch a couple of drunk kids just for talking trash."

"You didn't. You shoved them a little but you didn't throw the first punch. They did when they hit Mr. Coletti. You didn't start it, you just ended it, which was exactly what needed to be done. Exactly what a good cop would do."

Hunter was silent as Belle sniffed at a sand crab scuttling for something to eat. "A cop needs to know his brothers and sisters on the force have his back," he said quietly. "Mine didn't when I needed them most. I can't go back to the Salt Lake Police Department."

"So go somewhere else. The county sheriff's department can always use deputies or one of the smaller incorporated areas in the valley would probably love to have someone with your experience. Or you can even go further afield. If you were willing to move out of Salt Lake County, I'm sure there are a hundred small communities in the state who would be eager to add a seasoned veteran to their departments. Who knows, you might even find you prefer small-town crime fighting."

Hunter was stunned by the idea. He had been so consumed with anger at his department for not standing by him that he'd never even thought about moving to a different division.

"You also have an interesting perspective that most cops never get," Kate went on when he said nothing. "You know what it's like on the inside. I believe what happened to you—your wrongful conviction and imprisonment—would only make you a stronger detective, even more dedicated to finding justice. True justice, not just easy justice."

Hunter stared out to sea as her suggestion seemed to settle inside himself. Definitely something to think about.

He had thought his days as a cop were over. He had grieved over it but hadn't seen a way past his bitterness. He was angry at the system for failing him, but the bulk of his anger was against the officers and detectives he had worked with who had done a sloppy job investigating Dru's murder. They had focused on the most obvious suspect—him—and ignored any leads that pointed in other directions.

For the first time since his release, he felt a tiny flicker of hope that maybe he could move on, do something worthwhile with the rest of his life.

"What about you?" he asked Kate. "Where do you see yourself settling when your residency is done? Will you come back to Florida?"

The breeze off the Gulf lifted her hair, caressed her skin as he would like to be doing right about now. "I'm not sure what I'll do. I thought about returning to Central America for a while. There is so much work that needs to be done there. I don't know. With Utah's birthrate, there's always a need for family doctors in the state, especially in those smaller towns I was talking about."

"Cops and doctors can always find something to keep them busy, I suppose," he said.

"Unfortunately, sick people and crime seem to be universal."

"Well, wherever you decide to practice, your patients will be lucky to have you," he said gruffly.

She stopped walking and he could see her eyes soften in the moonlight. "Sometimes you say the sweetest things," she said. "Thank you."

Before he could tell her he meant every word, she leaned on tiptoe and kissed him.

They stood there in the sand with only their mouths connected and Hunter felt something deep and elemental shift inside him.

"Anyway, I don't want to think about the future or the past," Kate murmured. "For tonight, can we just focus on right now?"

He pulled her into his arms. *Right now* was just about the best moment of his life so he wasn't about to argue.

Chapter 13

Two days later, Kate woke sometime in the reverent hush before dawn. Outside the bedroom window, the sky was just beginning to lighten to a pale, silvery pink and the world seemed peaceful and still.

Hunter had pulled her to him sometime during the night and he slept on his side facing her, one arm casually flung across her rib cage.

With each breath, she could feel the soft brush of hair on his arms against her skin.

She could watch him sleep all day. At rest, he lost the hardness, the edginess, he wore as a shield against the world.

Really, when she thought about it, during this entire trip he had been lowering that protective shield inch by inch and letting the real Hunter out a little more.

These few days they had spent together in Key West had been so wonderful. It was as if all the dark shadows that had hovered around her since finding out about Charlotte McKinnon couldn't pierce the bright sunshine of the Key.

For two days, they laughed and talked and kissed and she had watched with delight as Hunter truly began to relax, as if he were slowly waking from a long, terrible nightmare.

She wanted to stay here forever, wrapped in this quiet, elusive peace—tangled together with him while the world outside this tropical paradise ceased to exist.

If only things were that simple. She could feel the pressure of all she had left behind begin to crowd in on her again. She shifted her gaze to the ceiling fan overhead, its plump leaf-shaped blades spinning slowly.

She had to face her past today. She had put it off too long but time was running out. Both of them needed to return to Utah. She had to start the next rotation of her residency bright and early Christmas morning, and Hunter needed to begin the process of picking up the pieces of his life.

She sighed, her heart already constricting at the pain she knew waited for her there.

She wasn't foolish enough to think they could remain in this idyllic bubble of passion and tenderness when they returned to the mountains and real life.

Hunter had given her no words of tenderness, had offered her nothing but the momentary comfort of his arms.

He was attracted to her, she had no doubt about that, and on some level he cared for her. She knew he did. But even when he made love to her, he kept a part of himself separate.

He didn't love her. She couldn't fool herself into thinking otherwise. No matter how she might wish it, she couldn't turn what they shared here into some kind of sweet happily-ever-after.

Lost in her thoughts, she was startled when she suddenly

felt a wet nose nudging at her. Belle stood on the other side of the bed, her eyes deep and mournful.

"You need to go out, honey?" she whispered. "Just a minute."

Though she hated leaving this warm, soft bed, she slipped out of Hunter's arms, holding her breath for fear she would wake him. A frown twisted those hard, lean features for a moment, then he rolled over.

Kate slipped on shorts and a T-shirt, found the pair of bright-purple flip-flops she had bought at a souvenir shop the day before and grabbed Belle's leash.

The hard-partying nights on Key West tended to make early mornings quiet. She didn't mind the lack of company at all as she and Belle walked down to the deserted beach. Kate enjoying the pale beginnings of sunrise while Belle marked her temporary territory then raced around for a while chasing the surf.

They walked until Belle's tongue lolled out from running and she started looking thirsty.

Back at the cottage, Kate made as little noise as possible while she filled the dog's water dish then carried it out to the porch.

She sat on the rocker, able to catch just a small glimpse of the surf through the lush growth.

"Next time, wake me up to take care of Belle."

Startled by the sudden deep voice, she turned to find Hunter standing in the doorway. He wore only a pair of jeans, the top button undone, and his hair was tousled from sleep, but she had never seen a more gorgeous sight.

She swallowed and tried to rearrange her suddenly scattered thoughts. "I didn't mind. I was up anyway. We took a little walk on the beach and watched the sunrise."

"I was worried when I woke and found you gone, until I

saw the empty crate and figured out Belle must have been bossing you around again."

"She's pretty good at getting her message across, isn't she?"

He returned her smile briefly, then turned serious. "I only reserved two nights here, Kate, which means we're supposed to check out today. I need to let the management know if we're staying longer."

She knew what he was asking. Though the sun was already climbing the sky, she was sure the morning suddenly seemed darker.

"It's time," she finally said. "Past time."

"Are you sure?"

She wasn't sure of anything except the inevitability of her heartbreak, but she forced herself to nod.

A strange light sparked in his eyes, one she couldn't read. He stood in the doorway looking strong and masculine and gorgeous.

"You won't be alone. I'll be right there with you."

She tried to smile. "I know."

He moved out onto the porch and pulled her to her feet and against that hard, wonderful chest. "We don't have to go yet," he murmured. "We still have a few hours."

She lifted her mouth for his kiss. The shadows could wait while they stayed in paradise a little longer.

For all her bravado earlier in the morning, Hunter could see Kate's nerves were stretched as thin as a strand of hair. She sat beside him with her hands folded tightly in her lap and her shoulders stiff as he drove the short distance from their bungalow to the Key West Terrace long-term care facility.

The building overlooked the Atlantic and was white brick

with terra-cotta roof tiles and a blooming tropical garden out front that gave it the look of a Mediterranean villa.

Though it was broad daylight, he could see holiday lights strung across the small gated yard. Inside, poinsettias in bright gold pots were arranged in a cone shape approximating a Christmas tree.

The tanned, perky young receptionist behind the glass information booth registered surprise when Kate asked for Brenda Golightly's room, as if not very many people asked that particular question.

"Are you friends or family?" she asked in a syrupy southern accent.

Kate seemed frozen by the question. She didn't answer, only gave him an anguished look that sliced at him worse than any prison shiv.

He stepped forward, his best charming-cop smile in place. "Something like that," he said.

The receptionist preened a little, like a turtledove. "Well, Ms. Golightly will be absolutely *thrilled* at the company, I'm sure. She's in the north wing, room 134. Just take the hallway to the left of the elevators. Follow that hall as far as it goes and Ms. Golightly's room is on the right. You can't miss it."

The halls had more holiday decorations, garlands of looped green and red paper, a smiling plastic Santa Claus pulling a sleigh and eight reindeer, and even a life-size poster of the Grinch.

Kate didn't appear to notice anything about their surroundings. The closer they walked to room 134, the more her color faded, until he was afraid she would disappear against the whitewashed walls.

He stopped outside a plain wood door devoid of ornamentation. "You don't have to put yourself through this, Kate. I can go in and interview her alone."

She seemed to steel her shoulders like a soldier heading into a firefight. "No. I appreciate the offer but I have to be there. I have to face her. After all these years, I *have* to."

Watching her battle her own fears was humbling and made him grieve for a blond little girl stolen from all she knew and thrust into a world where she knew no peace.

"Have I told you I think you're one of the strongest women I've ever met?" he asked, his voice low.

Her mouth parted a little in surprise but then he saw gratitude blossom in her eyes.

His words seemed to steady her, calm her. She drew in a deep breath and pushed open the door.

In contrast to the holiday gaiety in the hallway outside, room 134 was spartan, cheerless. His grandmother Bradshaw had spent the last year of her life in a nursing home. She'd died when he was in his early teens, but he remembered her room as an extension of the prissy, orderly house she had lived in before, with frilly doilies on the bedside table, lacy curtains and her favorite oil painting of a mountain sunset.

This room was like dozens of other hospital rooms he had seen in his life. Sterile, bland, and wholly lacking in personality.

A single bed with nobby blue institutional bedding dominated the room. A TV mounted high on the wall was playing a soap opera and the room smelled of antiseptic and the faint ammonia of urine.

The bed was empty. He wondered if they had come to the wrong room until he saw Kate's attention was focused on the window, where he now realized a woman sat in a wheelchair staring out.

She had dirty-blond hair with glaring bald patches. It wasn't unkempt, just long and unstyled. An oxygen line tethered her from a nasal cannula to the wall and she wore a sweat suit the color of kiwi fruit.

As he looked closer, he saw a face worn down by the grim ravages of time and a harsh life. She had a two-inch scar on her chin, a quarter-size pockmark on the other and she was missing a tooth.

There was a blankness to her features, an emptiness, and Hunter's heart sank.

Kate's brother was right, this was likely a wasted trip. How could this pitiful creature tell them anything?

Kate's eyes, blue and stormy, gave away some of her tumult as she stared at the faded shell of the woman she had both loved and hated. He saw she had reached the same grim conclusion he had—that their mission was doomed to failure—but still she drew a deep breath and walked into the room.

If he hadn't already loved her, he would have tumbled at that moment, hard and fast.

"Hello." Kate walked in and sat in one of the vinyl armchairs near the wheelchair.

Brenda Golightly narrowed her eyes then blinked rapidly several times as if coming awake from a long sleep. "Do I know you? I don't think I know you. Are you a new nurse? I don't like new nurses. Jane is my favorite nurse. She brings me extra pudding. Do you like pudding? I like pudding."

For all its singsong pitch, her voice was rough and raspy— from the oxygen or from her life choices, Hunter couldn't tell. Her speech was slightly slurred, rounded a little at the vowels.

At least she was verbal, he thought wryly, as she went on for several moments longer about her favorite kind of pudding.

He was certainly no developmental expert but she seemed

more like a child of seven or eight than a woman in her fifties. He found it rather disconcerting to hear inane, innocent chatter from someone who looked so world-weary and hardened.

After a moment, Kate put a hand on Brenda's knee to distract her from her soliloquy. "I'm not a new nurse. I…it's me. Kate. Katie."

At first, Hunter didn't see any visible reaction on Brenda's features and he wondered if she had even heard the words, then Brenda gave Kate a furtive, wary look out of the corner of her gaze.

After a moment, she gave a sharp, raspy laugh. "You're not *my* Katie! My Katie is little! You're all grown up."

Kate knotted her fingers together, obviously disconcerted.

"No." She cleared her throat, her eyes so distressed Hunter wanted to bundle her up and carry her out of here. "It's me, M-Mama. Katie."

Brenda smiled at something Hunter couldn't see. "I have a little girl named Katie. She's so pretty. Her hair is blonde like yours, but she's just a little girl. She likes pudding too. She has a doll named Barbara. Her doll has brown hair and freckles. I wish I had a doll named Barbara. Do you have any dolls?"

"Um, not anymore." Kate's attempt at a smile just about broke his heart. He couldn't stand the defeated devastation he saw in her eyes as she listened to Brenda and absorbed the true extent of her brain injury.

He saw all her hope for answers slip away like her childhood and he knew he couldn't sit by and watch it go.

He pasted on a smile he was far from feeling and stepped toward the two women, pulling a second armchair over to them.

"Hi, Brenda. I'm Hunter."

She studied him solemnly but said nothing. As he tried to formulate a strategy for questioning her, he noticed a couple of crayon drawings taped near the bed. Simple pictures of flowers and houses and trees, but he saw one that looked like a little girl with blond curly hair.

"Do you have any pictures of your little girl?"

He thought for a moment she wasn't going to answer him, then Brenda nodded. "I drew some."

He pointed toward the pictures by the bed. "Is that one?"

Her reserve melted like an ice-cream cone under the hot tropical sun and she nodded more vigorously.

"It's nice," he said.

"I have more. Do you want to see?"

"Sure."

She pointed him toward a drawer in the bedside table. He opened it and stared at the contents. Stacks and stacks of drawings showed the same little girl in a pink dress with yellow-crayon hair and huge blue eyes.

He took a few out and showed them to Kate, who looked stunned and baffled.

"These are very good."

"Told you she was pretty."

"You were right. Brenda, where is Katie?"

"Right there, in the pictures."

"No, where's the real Katie?" he asked gently.

Brenda blinked at him again then her eyes suddenly filled up with tears. "Gone. She's gone."

"Where?"

"They took her. It's not fair. They took her."

"Who took her?"

"The bad people. They said I wasn't a good mama but I was. I was!" The tears vanished as quickly as they had come. "I took care of her. I brushed her hair. I gave her animal crackers and dressed her in pretty pink clothes. I was a good mama but they took her and hid her from me."

Her eyes darted to his with a sly, sidelong look. "But I showed them. They hid her from me but I was smart and I found her. I found her and I stole her back."

Ah. Here it was. What they had traveled three thousand miles to learn. His heart pounding, he leaned forward. "Stole her back? How did you do that?"

She ignored his question, her eyes focused on Kate with such a fierce look of concentration Hunter wondered if somehow they were finally beginning to unwind the gauzy layers of memory. Maybe this damaged woman with her vague eyes and her worn-out body was beginning to reconcile the child to the woman.

Brenda stared at Kate for a long time, her dark eyes intense, then a radiant smile burst out, broken tooth and all. "Chocolate pudding is my favorite. What's yours?"

Kate's gaze shifted to his and the anguish in her eyes cut his heart to shreds. She swallowed hard a few times then mustered a grim facsimile of a smile. "Um, I like rice pudding. And tapioca."

Brenda rocked with sudden sharp laughter, one pale hand clapped over her mouth to contain her glee. "Ew. Tapioca tastes like fish eggs. I only like chocolate and banana."

Hunter broke in before she wandered off again about pudding. "You said you found Kate again," he said, trying to draw her back. "Where did you find her?"

Brenda didn't seem to mind his efforts to shepherd her through the conversation. She smoothed a finger over the construction-paper portrait, that hard, used-up face gentling a little. "They hid her from me but I always looked for her. You can't take a baby from her mama. It's wrong. Don't you think it's wrong?"

Hunter couldn't think how to answer that so he just nodded.

"Me, too. I looked and looked for her and one day I was driving my car and there she was. My little girl. My Katie." Her voice took on a defiant edge. "She was mine and they shouldn't have taken her so I took her back and we ran away where the bad people couldn't find us."

"But they did, didn't they?" Kate spoke up, her voice rough, strained. "She was taken away from you again, wasn't she? And this time you didn't want her back."

The sly defiance on Brenda's features just as quickly turned to anger. Her face suddenly turned an alarming puce and her thin, nearly concave chest started heaving violently. "Go away. I don't want you here. Go away! Where's my pudding? Where's Jane? I want my pudding!"

By the end she was nearly shouting, flailing her arms around violently, and Kate rose and laid a gentle hand on Brenda's arms.

"Okay. Okay," she murmured in a slow, nonthreatening voice she undoubtedly used with children in her medical practice. "We'll get you some pudding."

She had reached for Brenda's bony hand and it took Hunter a few moments to realize Kate was taking the woman's pulse.

"I think it's best if you rest now while we buzz for Jane, all right?"

Somehow Kate seemed to stow away her own distress at dredging up this painful past. Her voice was brisk, professional, but still calming. "Let's get you back into your bed now."

Hunter had never been very comfortable with strong emotion. The Judge certainly hadn't encouraged it in his only son. Bradshaw men were strong, stoic, invincible. They certainly weren't supposed to throw temper tantrums or—God forbid—shed tears about anything.

Hunter had made a conscious decision to follow his father's somewhat bloodless example rather than the wild pendulum of his mother's mood swings. Angela Bradshaw had enough strong emotions for all of them, with bitter, angry episodes or bone-deep depression followed with jarring, dizzying speed by frenetic gaiety.

Her bipolar disease had made his childhood unpredictable and precarious and he had never been sure when he came home from school whether she would smother him with kisses when he walked through the door or screech and yell at him for some infraction or other.

His father's way was safer. He had learned that even before the bitter humiliation of his arrest. In jail, he had done everything he could to shut off whatever stray emotions might flicker through him at odd moments. He couldn't afford to feel in prison, to show any sign of weakness, of fear or anger or bitterness. So he had shown nothing. Had become nothing.

But as he watched Kate carefully tuck in this woman who had brought her nothing but pain—who had stolen her from a happy, healthy home life and thrust her into a dark and terrifying world he could only imagine—all those emotions he had suppressed for so long rose up in his throat and threatened to choke him.

He was appalled at the burn of tears behind his eyes at her gentleness. He blinked them away, grateful Kate was too busy tending to Brenda to see the telltale sheen of moisture.

How could she do it? he wondered. Show compassion and kindness to the catalyst of her pain?

A nurse responded quickly to Kate's page. The infamous Jane of the extra pudding, she noted by her name tag. She was blond and round, in hospital scrubs printed with grinning cats.

"What's this now?" the nurse asked as she helped her transfer Brenda from the chair to the bed.

Though she wanted nothing more than to run out, away from this sterile room and this wild, tangled rush of emotions, Kate forced herself to focus on Brenda's physical symptoms.

"I'm afraid our visit has agitated her. I was concerned about her color and her pulse rate is nearly one-fifty."

"Oh dear. We can't have that now, can we?"

Kate watched the nurse tuck in the blankets, then pick up the crayon drawing Brenda had been showing them from the floor where she had dropped it in her frenzy.

She slipped it through Brenda's curled fingers and Kate was startled to see the silly, childlike crayon drawing seemed to have some kind of calming effect on Brenda.

Not sure how to identify the odd emotion tugging at her insides, Kate watched her clutch it like a talisman.

The nurse's voice was calm, soothing. "Take a nap now and when you wake up, you'll feel better, just in time for lunch."

Brenda nodded, obediently closing her eyes like a child expecting a birthday surprise when she opened them.

Kate didn't expect her to sleep but their visit must have sapped her energy reserves, obviously low. A moment later her breathing slowed and her thin chest began to rise and fall slowly.

The nurse waited until she slept, then picked up Brenda's chart off the end of the bed and made a few notations.

"How often does she have these episodes?" Kate asked.

The nurse's gentle demeanor with her patient turned cool

as she surveyed them. "I'm afraid federal privacy regulations prevent me from talking to you about her condition."

"I know all about HPAA. I'm a doctor."

"Not *her* doctor."

Kate drew a breath into lungs that felt tight and achy. "No," she agreed. "But I also know you can speak with immediate family. I'm her…"

She faltered, not quite knowing how to complete the sentence. "My name is Kate Spencer," she finally said. "But I legally changed it to that when I was eighteen. Before that, my name was Katie Golightly."

The nurse's eyes widened with shock, her arms going slack. "Oh my word! You're Katie! She talks about you all the time. I thought you were dead!"

Emotions crowded Kate, too many for her to handle at once. She pushed them all away for now. "No. I'm very much alive."

"And a doctor! She never said a word."

"Can you tell me about her condition? I know she had a TBI a few years ago but that doesn't account for all her symptoms."

Jane fidgeted with the chart but not before Kate saw evasiveness war with compassion. "Perhaps you should talk to her doctor. I'm sure Dr. Singh would have no problem with you studying her charts. He should be in this afternoon."

"I won't be here that long. We're just passing through."

That information apparently didn't sit well with the nurse. Her amazed expression gave way to disapproval. "I see."

She didn't. She couldn't possibly. How could this stranger understand the layers and layers of emotions here when Kate herself couldn't comprehend them?

She decided to try a different tack. "One of the first things

Brenda talked about when we arrived is how you're her favorite nurse. She said you give her extra pudding."

Jane's sudden coldness eased enough for her to smile a little. "It's just a little thing but it makes her happy. She does like her pudding."

"Please. You seem like a kind woman. All I'm asking is for a little information."

The nurse studied the drawing clutched in Brenda's hands then looked at Kate again. "She has cancer. Non-Hodgkins lymphoma."

She digested this and its implications. "AIDS?"

Jane's slow nod confirmed what Kate had already begun to suspect. Non-Hodgkins lymphoma, though it can appear in the regular population, had a greatly increased frequency in people infected with the AIDS virus.

She supposed she wasn't really surprised by the grim diagnosis. Brenda's lifestyle as a drug user and sometime prostitute made her a prime candidate to acquire the virus.

"Full blown," the nurse said, her brisk voice a contrast to the sadness in her eyes. "She's already had pneumococcal pneumonia twice this year. The cancer seems to be in remission for now but as I'm sure you know, it's very hard to control in AIDS patients. She could relapse any time. I'm very sorry to have to tell you this way."

Kate studied the wasted frame sleeping on the bed, suddenly awash with sorrow and regret for this woman who had lived such a hard life. What had led her down this road? she wondered, slightly ashamed of herself for never bothering to find out.

She knew very little about Brenda's history. Those weren't the kinds of questions a child asks a mother, especially one as unstable as Brenda, and as a teenager, she had been too angry and bitter at her for not letting the Spencers adopt her that it never would have occurred to her to dig into her past.

"Look, I'm going to give you my cell number and my pager number in Utah. Will you put it in her chart and have someone contact me when…when her condition changes?"

Jane looked at her for a moment, then to Kate's surprise she reached out and squeezed her fingers. "I will."

She bustled out of the room, leaving Kate and Hunter alone.

"Do you want to wait until Brenda wakes up and talk to her again?" Hunter asked after she left.

Kate touched the frail hand holding a crayon drawing, then lifted her gaze. "No. I don't want to upset her again. There's nothing for me here."

No answers to find and no one to blame.

Chapter 14

She was shutting him out, building walls around herself more effectively than all the concertina wire in the world.

Hunter's hands gripped the steering wheel as his Grand Cherokee rattled over yet another of Henry Flagler's bridges. Water surrounded them on both sides, stretching out as far as the eye could see. There might as well have been an ocean between him and Kate too, he thought.

She sat beside him, her face as composed and serene as a burial mask, but he knew damn well it was all an act. He had seen her eyes when they walked out of that nursing home, had seen the raw emotions in those lovely blue depths.

But somehow through the past hour she found a way to hide it all away while they picked Belle up from their cottage, checked out and headed through the merry holiday traffic away from Key West toward Miami.

Until they were on the road, she had kept up a steady stream of cheerful, light conversation. Every time he tried to draw the conversation back to Brenda and their interview with her, Kate either answered him with a monosyllable or ignored his question altogether, deliberately changing the subject.

She was shutting him out and he couldn't do a damn thing about it. Worse, he didn't have the first clue how to handle the hurt pulsing through him that she wouldn't let him reach her, even after all they had shared these last few days.

"You know, you can't keep doing this forever," he said suddenly.

He couldn't read her eyes behind her sunglasses but he saw one thin eyebrow arch above the curve of tortoiseshell plastic. "Keep doing what?"

"This game of duck and run. You'll have to talk about it sometime."

She leaned her head against the seat. "I know. But not yet. Please, Hunter."

How could he ignore that entreaty in her voice? He had certainly had plenty of experience burying his emotions down deep. If she wasn't ready to talk about what had happened with Brenda Golightly earlier, he wouldn't badger her.

"I don't remember when I've ever been so tired," Kate said as the tires spun along the raised highway. Would it bother you if I try to sleep for a while?"

"Of course not," he said, uncomfortable with the guilt pinching at him. Neither of them had slept much the last two nights. He couldn't seem to get enough of her—all she had to do was smile and he wanted her, with a fierce hunger that didn't ease even in the warm, peaceful aftermath of their love-making.

They would steal small slices of sleep but most of their nights—and days—had been spent in each other's arms.

Now Kate would barely look him in the eye, at least not without the buffer of her sunglasses. He tried not to feel hurt when she curled up on the seat, her back to him, but it sure as hell felt like a rejection.

Ignoring the sting and the deeper sense of loss at the apparent end to the closeness they had shared, he fiddled with the radio until he found something classical and relaxing.

"That's nice," she murmured with a soft smile over her shoulder. "Thank you. I don't need long. Wake me in an hour or so, would you?"

He didn't expect her to sleep. More likely she would feign sleep to prevent him from badgering her more about Brenda.

After a few miles with the gentle music and the low hum of the tires as her lullaby, soon Kate's breathing slowed and those slender knotted shoulders relaxed.

Good, he thought. She needed the rest. No matter what kind of bright, cheerful face she tried to put on it, he knew the visit to the nursing home had been draining for her.

He exhaled slowly. It hadn't exactly been a piece of cake for him either. Even the reading of the verdict in his trial hadn't seemed as stressful as the morning they had just endured, maybe because by the time the jury had rendered its verdict, Hunter had already resigned himself that conviction would be inevitable.

The case against him had been a strong one and public sentiment had run high that he was guilty.

What had they learned from Brenda Golightly? Kate would probably say nothing they didn't already know but in the past few hours Hunter's subconscious—the part of his brain that used to always be working a case even when he wasn't aware of it—had been busy formulating a theory.

From what little she said, he would bet his new SUV that she had given birth to a child named Katie Golightly around the same time Charlotte McKinnon had been born to Sam and Lynn McKinnon. Perhaps in Nevada, perhaps somewhere else. Kate had a birth certificate that showed her as being born to Brenda and an unnamed father so presumably a Katie Golightly once existed somewhere.

Judging by what Brenda had said, he surmised that the child had been taken away from her.

She was mine and they shouldn't have taken her so I took her back and we ran away where the bad people couldn't find us. That's what she had said.

He would talk to Gage McKinnon about following the paper trail to see if a child was removed from her custody in Nevada in the months prior to Charlotte McKinnon's kidnapping.

All this was speculation, but judging by the woman's history of substance abuse and borderline mental illness, he could guess she was probably high that fateful summer day when she happened to drive through the McKinnons' Las Vegas neighborhood.

She must have seen Charlotte playing in her yard. In a drug-induced psychosis, it would have been easy for her to convince herself the child was Katie Golightly, that she was only taking back what was hers.

Would this information give Kate any solace? He doubted it. But at least she might be able to reach some kind of understanding, a peace of sorts. Despite her problems, Brenda had obviously loved her daughter and grieved for her loss enough to try to take her back.

He shifted his gaze from the road for a moment to Kate's curved back. He had wanted so much to help her, to ease her tumult, and his failure gnawed at him.

Maybe if he could have helped her, some of his own sense of inadequacy would have dissipated a little. He had spent his time behind bars living each moment with the sobering knowledge that for all his skills as a detective, he had been powerless against the fates that conspired to put him on death row. This morning had been a grim reminder that for all his freedom now there were sometimes circumstances in life he couldn't control.

He couldn't control his feelings for Kate. Despite his better judgment—and his best effort—he had fallen in love with her, for all the good it did him. He planned to keep that little nugget of information to himself.

The last thing she needed right now was another snarl in an already tangled life.

She was having a tough enough time coming to terms with her past. He wouldn't complicate things even more for her. With all she had on her plate, she didn't need a bitter ex-con with a hazy future stepping up to clutter her life, too.

As he drove north, he couldn't help feeling like he was leaving behind warmth and sunshine and heading back into the cold.

She dreamed she was three years old again, her chubby legs planted on a wide grassy field, with the sun bright in her eyes and the world brimming with joy.

She couldn't decide what to do first, somersault across the field or twirl around, arms out and her frilly pink skirt flying high, until she was so dizzy she fell over in a heap.

She started to clap her hands with glee, then she realized instead of arms and hands she had thick braided ropes at the end of her shoulders that she could only wave helplessly.

Suddenly she found herself surrounded by all the players in the drama of her life. The McKinnons—Sam, Lynn and much younger version of Gage and Wyatt—stood on one side while on the other were Maryanne and Tom Spencer, along with her two best friends from junior high school and Mr. Moffat, her high school science teacher, of all people.

A whistle blew somewhere and an instant later Kate felt a tug on her rope-arms and found herself in the middle of a deadly serious battle of tug-of-war. Her shoulders were nearly dislocated as both teams did their best to pull her to their side.

She cried out for them to stop but no one seemed to be paying the slightest bit of attention to her. Neither side seemed to be gaining an advantage but their efforts were fierce.

At last, when she wasn't sure she could stand another moment, a woman with dirty blonde hair and a missing front tooth wheeled out onto the grassy field.

Right there in the middle of the game she picked up Kate, rope arms and all, piled her onto her lap and rolled off the field away from all the players, with Kate screaming and crying out for her to stop....

"Kate? Everything okay?"

The deep voice intruded into her nightmare and Kate woke with a start, the coppery taste of blood in her mouth. It took her a few seconds to realize she must have bitten her lip in her sleep.

She was disoriented for a moment, trapped there in that odd, surreal place between sleep and consciousness.

"You were dreaming. Must have been a doozy. You were crying out."

She found Hunter watching her, his eyes solemn and concerned, and his lean, familiar features calmed her.

Right. They were in his SUV again, heading northwest, back to Utah and the McKinnons, where she belonged.

"I'm all right now," she said, dabbing her lip with a tissue from the console.

"What were you dreaming?"

"Nothing. I don't remember." She ignored her qualm over the lie. "Where are we?"

"A ways past Fort Myers," Hunter replied. "We should be in St. Petersburg by dinnertime."

She straightened. "St. Petersburg?"

"I told you we could stop in and visit the Spencers while we're in Florida. Give you a chance to drop off those presents you bought them in Key West. We can even stay for a day or two if you'd like."

To her horror, hot tears burned her eyes. How could such a hard, unrelenting man have these astonishing bouts of kindness? She blinked back her tears, knowing they would only embarrass them both. "Thank you, Hunter."

He shrugged off her gratitude, as he had been doing all week whenever she tried to tell him how much his help meant to her.

"I'd like to meet them anyway," he said, his voice gruff. "They sound like remarkable people."

Suddenly she was aware of a deep hunger to see her foster parents, to wrap her arms around Tom's comfortable bulk and find center again in Maryanne's calm, eternally serene expression. It suddenly seemed like exactly the place she needed to be.

"They are wonderful. You'll like them and I know they'll like you."

"Prison record and all?"

She narrowed her gaze at him. "You don't have a record. It was expunged."

"Right." He gave that self-mocking smile she hated, the one she realized she hadn't seen for a while. "Too bad I can't expunge the last three years so easily."

She hadn't heard that grim note to his voice for several days either. Its return left her inexpressibly sad. She had hoped he was moving past his anger at what had happened to him.

"If we've made it past this far, I must have been sleeping for hours," she murmured. "Through Miami and Ft. Lauderdale and Alligator Alley. You should have woke me."

"You needed the rest."

She hadn't been getting much sleep the last few nights. The reason why sat next to her in the driver's seat, just a hint of afternoon shadow stubbling his jaw. He looked big and powerful and incredibly sexy, even with the hardness in his eyes.

She hadn't *wanted* to sleep much the last few nights, not when she was exactly where she needed to be, wrapped in his arms.

She had a fierce sudden desire to be there again, to feel him around her and inside her again, and wondered with a pang if she would ever have the chance.

A muscle flexed in his jaw suddenly and she wondered if could somehow guess the direction of her thoughts. Color soaked her cheeks and she pretended extreme interest in the passing scenery.

"Do you feel better?" Hunter asked at her silence.

She thought of that terrible dream, the horrible sensation that she was being torn apart.

"I don't know," she admitted. "Physically, yes."

She didn't add that emotionally her psyche felt as battered and bloody as the gang members she treated after a nasty street fight.

Maybe she didn't need to share that information with him. The way he looked at her, his eyes fathomless and dark, she thought maybe he already knew.

After nearly a week on the road, Hunter likely knew her better than anyone else in the world. She found it an alarming realization, especially as she wasn't even sure she knew herself anymore.

"I should probably stop for gas soon," he said.

"I imagine Belle could use a good run."

"Yeah, probably." He took the next exit where a cluster of gas stations squatted in the sun.

"Do me a favor, will you?"

She looked at him quizzically.

"Try not to get into trouble while we're here. No more adventures. No pregnant women ready to pop, no blind men who need a lift to Memphis, no drunk college boys looking for a little action. Let's just make this a simple pit stop, okay?"

She laughed a little, as she realized he had intended. "I'll do my best. Although I'll remind you I had nothing to do with the college boys. That was all you, detective."

As if their time together in Key West had altered their established pattern, this time Kate insisted on pumping the gas so that Hunter could exercise Belle.

"You've been driving the whole time I slept so you deserve a little rest," she told him firmly.

After a small argument, Hunter finally ceded defeat and grabbed Belle's leash and a ball then headed toward a grassy field next to the filling station.

Kate finished filling the tank, then wandered over to watch them. This was another of those moments she would store in her memory bank. The pure joy of a gleeful dog and her master at play.

How many more moments like this would she have? In a few days they would be home and would go their separate ways. She would still see him, she had no doubt of that. His sister was her best friend so it was inevitable that the paths of their respective lives would intersect again but nothing would be the same.

She wouldn't think about it, she decided as sadness slipped over her like clouds over the sun. It would be foolish to waste their few remaining days together worrying about the inevitable pain of their parting.

What if they didn't have to part? The thought, insidious and seductive, slithered across her mind. What if she walked right over to him, took his face in her hands and told him she was hopelessly in love with him?

No. She couldn't do that to him. He didn't share her feelings and she wouldn't burden him with them.

He deserved a woman who was whole and healthy, not someone fractured and damaged, someone desperately afraid the broken pieces of herself would never come together again.

The moment Hunter drove down the quiet street in a comfortably middle-class St. Petersburg neighborhood and parked in front of the dearly familiar rose brick house, Kate felt some of those stray pieces of herself start jostling back into place.

She loved this place. From the hanging begonias on the front porch to the carefully tended lawn to the colorful Christmas lights Tom insisted on stringing across all available surfaces every year.

She jumped from the car, ready to race up and fling open the door like a child racing home from school, but she forced herself to wait with hard-won patience for Hunter to let Belle out of her crate and leash her before she hurried up the walkway with him.

Though it felt odd to ring the doorbell of the house she

had spent so much of her life in, she didn't feel right about bursting in when they weren't expecting her.

Long moments passed while they waited for someone to answer, until she began to have the horrible fear that perhaps they weren't home.

Maybe they were traveling. She had spoken with Maryanne a few days before Wyatt and Taylor's wedding the week before and she hadn't said a word about going anywhere, but Tom was in the habit of coming home from work with itchy feet and dragging Maryanne on one of their impromptu jaunts across the South.

It seemed desperately important that they be home. She held her breath and only let it out when she heard yipping behind the door. Their little shitzu Lily was a fierce guard dog, even if she only weighed about fifteen pounds.

A moment later she heard a deep voice ordering her to be quiet, for the love of Pete, and a moment later the door swung open.

Her foster father stared out at her for just an instant. Then his broad, handsome face lit up with joy.

"Pumpkin? What on earth?"

He opened his arms and she walked into them, closing her eyes to savor the distinctive scents of wintergreen Life-Savers and Old Spice.

He held her close, rocking a little in the doorway, while Lily and Belle sniffed each other.

"How's my favorite doctor?"

She smiled against his broad, sturdy chest. "Great. How's mine?"

"Couldn't be better, especially since my best girl's come home." He pulled away long enough to call down the hallway.

"Maryanne, you better come on out and see who's come a-knocking."

A moment later, Maryanne walked in wiping her hands on her favorite apron, one Kate had sewed for her years ago in home economics.

When she caught sight of Kate in the doorway, amazement leaped into those calm brown eyes and she gasped with delight. "Katie? Oh, darling, what a wonderful surprise!"

She pulled her from Tom's arms and wrapped her arms tightly. Kate hugged her back, barely able to breathe through the love coursing through her for these people who had taken her in and given her a chance.

Though they had talked several times since she learned the results of that DNA test confirming she was Charlotte McKinnon, she hadn't seen them since. Now, wrapped in the arms of their love, she finally realized how afraid she had been about this moment. Deep in her heart, she had been dreadfully afraid things had been forever changed between them.

She needn't have worried.

"Oh, I can't tell you how marvelous it is to see you!" Maryanne pressed her warm cheek to Kate's. "But what are you doing here? I thought you said last week you weren't going to be able to come for Christmas."

"I can't stay that long. I'm starting my newborn ICU rotation Christmas morning."

Disappointment flickered in those brown eyes but Maryanne squeezed her hands. "Well, you're here now and that's the important thing. You'll stay the night, of course. You and your friend."

Hunter! Kate stepped back, appalled at her horrible manners. She had left Hunter and Belle standing on the porch during her happy reunion with the Spencers.

She pulled him inside, noting immediately that Belle and Lily had rekindled their friendship begun a few years ago when the Spencers came out to Utah for an impromptu ski trip.

"I'm sorry. Tom, Maryanne, this is Hunter Bradshaw, Taylor's brother. And of course you remember Belle."

She had been a little nervous at their reaction to Hunter but again, she should have known better. Tom reached around her and shook Hunter's hand.

"Mr. Bradshaw. It's a real pleasure. We've heard a lot about you."

Hunter looked a little disconcerted at that information and sent Kate a questioning look.

To her dismay, she could feel herself blush. "Taylor," she explained quickly. "Tom and Maryanne met her when they came to Utah to visit and then she and I drove out here together a few years ago."

"Right."

"Come in, come in," Maryanne said. "I was just getting ready to fry up some chicken. I was making extra for Tom's lunch later in the week so there's plenty for both of you."

"Do I have time to walk the dog first before dinner?" Hunter asked.

"Why, of course," Maryanne answered with Southern politeness. "Will half an hour give you enough time?"

He nodded and Tom grabbed Lily's leash off its hook by the door. "Mind some company?" he asked.

Hunter looked a little uncomfortable at the idea but he shook his head.

"Good," Tom said with a smile. "While Maryanne works her usual magic in the kitchen, you can tell me what brings you both all this way."

Kate watched them go, praying fiercely that Tom wouldn't pull his concerned-father routine and subject Hunter to the third-degree.

She watched them walk to the end of the driveway and head west before she followed Maryanne into the kitchen.

The familiar smells and sights in the room seemed to instantly transport her to her teenage years, sitting at the bar, dipping graham crackers in milk and telling Maryanne about her day while they waited for Tom to come home so he could help her with her Trig homework.

"It's so good to be here," she told Maryanne truthfully.

"Now what's this all about? What are you doing in Florida? And with Taylor's brother, of all people."

Kate took her usual stool at the bar, not sure where to begin. She finally cut to the heart of the matter.

"Looking for Brenda."

"Oh baby." Maryanne looked up from dipping the chicken pieces in her special blend, her eyes deep and dark with compassion. "What were you hoping to find?"

"Why she did it. Why me instead of some other poor little girl. I had to try to find out. I *had* to. It was Hunter's idea but as soon as he offered to search for her, I knew this was something I had to do."

"Did you find her?"

Kate gripped both hands around Maryanne's ever-present cup of tea. "Yes. She's in a Key West nursing home after a drug overdose a few years ago. She's in bad shape with AIDS-related cancer and the overdose left her with lasting brain damage."

Maryanne frowned. "So you weren't able to find any answers."

She thought of the little they had learned, of those few tantalizing moments when she thought Brenda recognized her and was ready to tell all. "Not what I was hoping for, anyway."

"How did you feel, seeing her?"

Her foster mother was always asking questions like that, forcing Kate to examine her actions and reactions. She should have been a shrink, Kate thought.

How did winning that geography bee make you feel? Why do you think you made that kind of decision to break curfew? How could you have handled the conflict with your English teacher better?

The third degree used to drive her crazy but now she recognized it for what it was; Maryanne's not-so-subtle method of helping a troubled, confused young girl learn to sort through her wild jumble of emotions to find the truly important ones.

"I don't hate her. I thought I did—from about the third or fourth time she refused to give up her parental rights so you could adopt me, I thought I hated her. You know I did. I expected to feel that hot, familiar weight of it as I walked into her room. But seeing her lying there so frail and worn-out, I felt nothing. Nothing but sadness."

Maryanne appeared to think about this as she added the chicken to the oil. The kitchen was filled with their merry sizzle and delicious scent before she finally spoke.

"You know, the other day I lost my car keys. While I was searching the house for them, I accidentally discovered—to my considerable dismay, you can be sure—that the diamond had fallen out of my wedding ring setting. The big one. I only realized it when I happened to see something glittering on the dresser in the bedroom while I was there searching the room for my keys. If I hadn't been scatter-brained enough to lose my keys in the first place and go looking for them, who knows when I would have realized that diamond was missing and where it would have ended up by then?"

Her gaze met Kate's and she smiled. "Life is funny that

way. Sometimes we think we're looking for one thing when, really, what we end up finding is something else entirely. Something we never even realized was missing."

That was something else Maryanne was always doing. She seemed to have a parable for everything, from losing a soccer game to learning the correct way to sort laundry.

"What's that supposed to mean?"

"You think about it. What do you think is more important? Finding out why things happened to you or learning to find peace with it even if you never know the reasons?"

Before she could puzzle this out, she heard the bustle of two men and two dogs returning through the front door.

"Hope that chicken is almost done," Tom said as they walked into the kitchen. "That smells enough to bring a man to his knees. Isn't that right, Bradshaw?"

"Absolutely." A corner of Hunter's mouth quirked up and Kate's heart turned over with love for him.

She may not have found answers or peace on this trip but she had certainly found her own treasure, better than a loose diamond. Too bad she wouldn't be able to keep it.

Chapter 15

Hunter couldn't sleep.

He found that odd, really, because the Spencers' guest room was the most comfortably, cozy space he had inhabited for a long time. With a bed as wide and deep as a mountain lake, crisp, cool cotton sheets and a stack of paperbacks by the bed, he should have been completely content.

But his arms felt empty and familiar restlessness prowled through him.

He missed Kate.

She was the reason he had wandered the guest room for the last two hours, until he knew every inch of it. The discovery wasn't a pleasant one. Though he had only spent two glorious days with Kate in his arms and his bed, the prospect of a night without her left him hollow.

What worried him most was that making love to her wasn't the thing he missed most, but those priceless, peaceful moments he held her while she slept, tenderness a sweet, heavy ache in his chest.

"Damn, I've got it bad," he said out loud.

Belle, curled up on the floor, blinked at him sleepily then snuffled and went back to sleep.

Hunter sighed and wandered to the window again. Outside in the Spencers' backyard, their pool gleamed blue in the moonlight, cool and inviting. If he had brought a suit along he would have worked some of this restlessness off with a good hard swim.

He was almost tempted to go out anyway, but since he didn't relish the idea of Kate's foster parents wandering out to find him skinny-dipping in their swimming pool, he discarded the idea.

He liked Tom and Maryanne Spencer. They seemed genuinely good people, the kind of grounded souls who calmed everyone lucky enough to wander into their sphere.

On their walk earlier with the dog, he had been sure Tom would grill him, the kind of paternal interrogation a father subjects to any man who drags his daughter across the country.

He braced himself, waiting for Tom Spencer to bring up his prison time—or at least ask if he was sleeping with Kate. But the good doctor only asked about the weather on their trip, what kind of highway mileage his Grand Cherokee got, if they had visited any maritime museums when they were in the Keys.

Only as they turned around and started back toward the house did he ask in a quiet, calm voice how Hunter was adjusting to the world after his incarceration.

Hunter had almost brushed him off with a curt answer but something had compelled him to tell Tom Spencer the truth.

"It's a struggle," he had admitted to Kate's foster father. "But every day seems a little easier."

Tom had smiled and patted him on the shoulder as if Hunter were seven years old. "You're going to be fine, son. Just fine."

The strange thing was, for the first time in a long time, Hunter almost believed him. He kept thinking about Henry Monroe's words earlier in the week, about having a choice to make when he started to go blind.

I could sit there in my house until I died, scared and angry and bitter. Or I could go on living. I decided to go on.

He needed to make that choice, too, but he didn't know how.

Dinner had been enjoyable, he remembered now as he gazed out at the play of moonlight on water. Maryanne's fried chicken had been perfect, crispy and spicy and melt-in-your-mouth delicious. The conversation had jumped all over the place but through it all he had sensed the deep love running like a river through that dining room.

Kate adored them and they obviously returned her affection.

Hunter had never considered himself a touchy-feely kind of person but throughout the evening they spent together he had wanted to grab both Maryanne and Tom in a tight hug and thank them for rescuing a scared, troubled young girl.

With another sigh, he traced a finger down the window. What the hell was he going to do about Kate?

He thought of the courage it must have taken for her to walk into that room at the nursing home earlier that day. It humbled him. She was brave enough to face her fears yet he cowered here, afraid to tell her how much he loved her.

That was the crux of the matter. He had been telling himself since that day on the beach when he realized he had fallen headlong for her that keeping quiet about his feelings was some kind of high-minded, magnanimous gesture. She deserved better, he had told himself.

That hadn't been the issue at all. He faced that now, just past midnight, alone in his room. Really, it all came down to a choice, just like Henry had talked about.

A choice he still wasn't sure he was capable of making.

To reach for Kate and the happiness and contentment that beckoned with her, he would have to let go of all the ugliness, all the hate. There wasn't room in his life and his heart for both.

Was he strong enough to make that choice—to release his anger and bitterness over Martin James and the lives he had taken, the time he had stolen from Hunter—so he could grab hold of something better?

He didn't know. That was the hell of it. So he holed out here in this comfortable guest room, exhaustion seeping through him, more lonely than he had been, even during those dark nights at the Point of the Mountain.

He was just about to give up and toss and turn in the bed for a while when he saw movement out in the lovely yard, a dark shadow slipping out of the house and wandering toward the pool.

Kate.

In the pale, clouded moonlight, he saw she was dressed in a gauzy white nightgown and looked fragile, otherworldly, like something off the cover of one of those spooky haunted-mansion-type novels his sister used to read.

His heart seemed to twist in his chest as he watched her standing by the pool, gazing up at the stars.

The urge to go to her blew through him like a hurricane but he didn't dare. Until he figured out whether he was ready to live again, he would be best to keep his distance.

He would have stayed in his guest room and tried to sleep if the moon hadn't slipped from behind the clouds and captured her features in pale moonlight.

The twist of emotions there broke his heart.

Without taking time to think through the consequences, Hunter made his silent way through the house and out into the quiet backyard.

Kate looked up when he opened the door but said nothing as he approached.

"Nice night," he murmured.

"In a few days we'll be back to single-digit temperatures and whiteouts. I figured I had better enjoy a pleasant night while I have the chance since we won't see one in Utah until June."

"Mind if I join you?"

She gestured to the plastic chaise lounge next to her and they both sat there, gazing up at the stars.

"You ready to talk about things yet?" he asked after a moment.

She didn't say anything for a full thirty seconds. "What time is it?" she finally said.

Disappointment flickered through him at what he thought was another attempt to change the subject.

"About half past midnight."

"It's officially my birthday then."

He stared. "Why didn't you say something? Or the Spencers? They didn't say a word about it all evening. I would have thought Maryanne would have at least whipped up a cake for you."

"They probably don't even know."

"How could they not know it's your birthday?" he asked with a frown.

"December 19 is Charlotte McKinnon's birthday. I only learned that little bit of information after Gage and Wyatt found me. I've always celebrated my birthday on March 16. That's the date on my birth certificate. On Katie Golightly's birth certificate, I should say. I'm three months older than I always thought I was. Funny, isn't it?"

He found the whole thing remarkably unamusing, especially when her last word came out more like a sob.

He couldn't bear it, any more than he could sit by and do nothing. He rose and tugged her into his arms, then sat again with her on his lap.

She stayed frozen in his arms briefly, her spine rigid and her shoulders tight, then she seemed to sag against him. Her arms slid around him and she held on tight while a storm of tears buffeted her.

"I'm sorry," she murmured after several moments of silent weeping. "I'm so sorry, Hunter. I didn't mean to cry all over you again. I feel like all I've done for six weeks is bawl."

Her forced laugh turned into another sob. "I hate this, Hunter. I hate it."

She punched his chest for emphasis and he folded her small fist inside his hand. "I know you do. Anyone would."

"I've always refused to think of myself as a victim. It was important to me. Maybe I went through some ugly stuff when I was a kid. But then, who didn't? I survived it. More than survived it, I've built a good life for myself and I'm doing something I love, helping others. I don't want to feel like a victim but I can't seem to help it."

"You were a victim. You can't change that. You were three years old with no control at all over the situation."

"I thought seeing her today would, I don't know, give me some kind of peace. Closure. But nothing has changed. I still don't know who I am. What I am. I feel like I'm three people wrapped up in one royally screwed-up package. Which is it? Am I Katie Golightly, the poor, pitiful little girl abandoned by her junkie whore of a mother? Or Kate Spencer,

M.D., beloved foster daughter of Tom and Maryanne Spencer? And where does Charlotte McKinnon and her family fit into the mix? I just don't know!"

He kissed the top of her head, love and tenderness and compassion thick in his chest. This was it, then. What he had been running from these last few days. His fears seemed insignificant compared to the need to comfort her, to try to ease her pain.

"You're all those things, Kate. All those things and more."

She made a sound of disbelief and he tightened his arms. "I know who you are. You're a smart, compassionate, beautiful woman. All those things you've been through that you want to discount have made you the person you are today."

"A mess?" She meant the words as a little self-deprecating joke but Hunter didn't laugh. Instead, he continued to hold her tightly, gazing at her with the moon shooting sparks of light through his dark hair and an intense expression in his eyes.

"A woman of great courage and strength," he said quietly. "A woman who can't sit by and do nothing when she sees anyone else in pain, whether that pain is physical or emotional."

She drew in a shaky breath, stunned by his words. "Is that really how you see me?"

He studied her, that muscle working his jaw. "Do you want to know what I see when I look at you?"

She nodded, holding her breath as her stomach suddenly jumped with nerves.

"I see a woman with every reason to hate but with this great core of love inside her. A woman who somehow found the strength of character to show the frail, broken-down shell of her kidnapper nothing but compassion and gentleness."

She let out her breath, warmth spreading through her as he went on.

"I've seen so much ugliness in my life, Kate. Parents torturing children, husbands killing wives. It's all part of a cop's life. You learn to deal with it in your own way but it still gets to you, grinds away at your spirit. And then for eighteen months I lived with men who committed crimes heinous enough to put them on death row. Murderers, rapists. Child molesters. The worst of the worst. It's enough to shake a person's faith that there's anything good and decent left in the world."

His arms tightened and she felt the light, feather-soft brush of his mouth against her hair again.

"On this trip, because of you, I've found that faith again. What I saw in that nursing home was beautiful. The most beautiful thing I've ever seen. And it wasn't just that moment. I saw you show the same loving, healing care to a frightened mother giving birth under less than perfect circumstances and to a frail old man trying to make it to see his granddaughter dance, even though he couldn't see anything at all."

"You helped Mariah and Henry too," she was compelled to remind him.

"Only because you pushed me into it. On this trip you've made me better than I am, Kate. I don't know if it's because of what happened to you or in spite of it but you're amazing."

He rubbed a thumb over her cheek and the tenderness of the gesture weakened her knees. She wanted to close her eyes and lean into him, to stay right here in his arms.

"You're amazing," he repeated. "How could I help but fall in love with you?"

His words didn't register at first but when they did she

jerked her eyes open and jumped to her feet. "What? You *what?*"

He laughed at her stunned reaction. "I know. Shocked the heck out of me too. I wasn't looking for it but there it is. I love you, Katie Golightly, Kate Spencer, Charlotte McKinnon. Whoever you are, I love you."

She couldn't think, couldn't breathe, could only stand there on a moonlit Florida night and stare at him. "You can't love me!"

"And yet I do."

"How can you possibly, after I dragged you across the country on this wild goose chase and have spent the whole week moaning and complaining about my poor, pitiful life?"

He laughed again and reached for her hand. His fingers caressed hers and sent twirly, twitchy little nerve impulses up her arm. "Oh, I wouldn't say that's all you've done."

Heat soaked her cheeks as she remembered trying to seduce him, as she thought of the passion they shared and her own voraciousness.

The impact of his words finally fully hit her and she sank down onto the chaise lounge again.

"You love me."

"I said so, didn't I? Why is it so hard for you to believe?"

"I never thought I would hear you say that. I…I suppose I can't believe it because I've loved you forever," she finally admitted and had the satisfaction of seeing him blink in surprise.

"You have not."

"Well, at least since the first day we met, when you were sitting in that diner with those cops. I remember it vividly. It was the middle of the night and Taylor and I walked in after studying and you were so thrilled to see her. I never had a brother and seeing how much you obviously adored your little sister was the first thing I loved about you. The more I learned about you, the more I came to love."

He reached for her and kissed her, and the emotion behind it had tears stinging her eyes again.

Several moments later, they were both breathing heavily and her body shimmered with tenderness and desire, all the more acute because she knew they couldn't act on it. Not tonight, while they were guests in her parents' house.

With a groan that told her he was every bit as aroused as she—and understood it couldn't lead anywhere tonight—Hunter wrenched his mouth from hers. "We have to stop now or I won't be able to."

There would be other moments, she thought as joy winged its way through her. Moments when they would be free to touch and taste and explore. That knowledge lent an edge of sweet anticipation to her frustration.

"If you loved me for so long," Hunter said gruffly, "why didn't you say anything?"

She shrugged. "A few reasons. Dru, for one thing. She was a biggie. You started dating her right around that time and a few months later she announced to the world she was pregnant. You were trying to get her to marry you and I was so angry with her for the way she acted I wanted to punch out her pretty white teeth."

She grew quiet. "And then she was killed," she said softly.

"And I was arrested and charged with her murder. I don't blame you for wanting nothing to do with a convicted felon."

"That had nothing to do with it! Nothing. I never once believed you were guilty. You know that. I would have poured out my feelings at any moment to you but you didn't even want your sister to visit you in prison. How could I suddenly show up with some story about how I was crazy about you? I would have looked like those desperate women who suddenly claim undying love for men behind bars."

They were both silent as Kate pondered the amazing twists and turns in their lives that had led them here, to this moment.

"So what now?" he asked. "I've never done this before so I'm not quite sure what comes next."

She linked her hands through his. Here it was, then, the peace she had traveled across the country to find. They had both been through tough times, but somehow they had managed to come through the other side to find each other.

"Let's go home," she said.

Epilogue

"Are you sure you're up to this?"

Six days later, Christmas eve, they sat in Hunter's Grand Cherokee gazing out at Lynn McKinnon's cedar-and-glass house, smoke curling from the chimney and Christmas lights gleaming merrily through the fluttery snow.

Full circle, she thought.

Two weeks earlier they had stood together on Hunter's deck while mountain snow swirled around them and now here they were back under the same conditions.

The same weather, maybe. But everything else had changed.

She squeezed his fingers. "Lynn's expecting us. I don't want to hurt her feelings."

"I'm sure she would understand. You're exhausted from all that traveling."

She laughed. "Right. The traveling. That's it."

He looked slightly abashed, which only made her laugh more. They had spent six days on the road, wending their way slowly from Florida to Utah. They probably could have made the journey in half the time barring complications like they encountered on the way east, but neither of them had been in much of a hurry.

They rose late each morning, still warm and sated from a night spent in each other's arms, then drove until they were tired enough—or hungry enough for each other—that they stopped again for more.

How different their return journey had been! With the simmering tension between them gone and their feelings out in the open, Kate had found every moment one of pure delight, whether they were laughing about a bumper sticker on an eighteen-wheeler or watching Belle chase a ball through the snow in Wyoming, where they had spent the previous night.

She loved Hunter more after those six wonderful days than she ever believed possible.

Part of her would rather go home with him and spend this most magical of nights in his arms, at his quiet mountain home where everything had begun.

But she couldn't deny the surprising discovery that her heart beat with eagerness to walk inside Lynn's beautiful home and see again the people she knew waited for her there.

"I'm ready," she murmured.

Hunter climbed out and came around to open her door, then piled his arms with the presents loaded onto the back seat. They had barely had time to stop at her apartment in Salt Lake City to drop Belle off and pick up her stash of gifts. Kate could only be grateful she had been neurotic enough to wrap all but the ones they bought in Florida before she left—and she had paid extra for gift wrap on all those last-minute purchases.

Soft snowflakes drifted around them as they walked up the sidewalk together. Just for old time's sake she stuck her tongue out to catch a few, earning a laugh from Hunter.

Kate freed a hand from the packages she carried to ring the doorbell, and a few moments later Gage's oldest stepdaughter, Gabriella, opened the door, her gamine little face lighting up when she saw them.

"Aunt Kate! Aunt Kate! You're here! That means we can open presents now!"

Aunt Kate. My word. Kate wasn't quite sure how she felt about that one. She didn't have time to sort it out before Gaby raced off, most likely to find her younger sister and partner in crime.

She and Hunter stood in the doorway for a moment, then looked at each other and laughed when no one else came to greet them.

Through the entryway, Kate could hear voices and soft holiday music so she decided just to walk in. She belonged here, after all, whether she was ready to accept that or not.

Laughter and heat and delicious smells assailed them when they walked into Lynn's comfortable-sized gathering room. Pine, roast turkey and some kind of pie—possibly cinnamon apple—were the dominant scents.

No one seemed to notice their entrance and Kate took the opportunity to study this family she was slowly coming to know.

Wyatt and Taylor were nowhere to be found, but Gage and Allie sat on one of the pair of plump burgundy couches arranged around a river-rock fireplace that crackled merrily. They were holding hands, she saw, as they admired the wrapped presents under the tree with Allie's daughters, who seemed to be pawing through each one for any that might have their names on them.

Kate's gaze found Lynn and Sam standing together in the open kitchen. Lynn wore a holiday-print apron and her lovely face glowed pink. Probably from working in the kitchen all day, Kate thought, judging by the delicious-looking feast spread on the table; then she saw Sam sneak a kiss on the back of his ex-wife's neck exposed by her graceful French braid.

Well, well! This was an interesting development. Sam and Lynn had been divorced since shortly after her kidnapping and neither of them had ever remarried. Wouldn't it be something if they could rekindle their relationship now, after all the years and pain?

As if drawn by radar, Lynn suddenly looked up and found them standing there. She flushed even brighter and stepped away from Sam.

"Kate! You're back."

"Just barely. I only stopped home to drop off my luggage."

"I was so afraid you wouldn't make it in time. Oh, I'm so glad you're here!"

She dropped the wooden spoon she held and rushed forward. Kate barely had time to hand her presents into Hunter's already burdened arms before Lynn swept her into a cinnamon-scented embrace.

As her mother pressed a soft cheek to hers, Kate waited for the familiar discomfort to pinch her at Lynn's eager affection, but she couldn't seem to find it anywhere. Instead, she returned Lynn's embrace, warm affection bubbling up inside her like eggnog.

Sam joined them and Lynn handed her over to him. Again Kate was startled by the contentment stealing over her.

"Do you want the presents under the tree?" she heard Hunter ask Lynn.

"That would be fine, dear."

He left her side long enough to put their packages along with the rest, to the delight of Gaby and Anna.

"Hunter came with me. I hope you don't mind."

"Of course not!" Lynn assured her. "He's Taylor's brother so that makes him practically one of the family."

And soon he would be more, Kate thought, joy pulsing through her again, but she held that secret close to her heart for now.

"Dinner's almost ready. I'm just taking the rolls out of the oven."

"How can I help?" Kate asked as Hunter rejoined her.

"I've got it. Just sit down and visit with your brothers."

"I see Gage but where's Wyatt? Did we beat them here?"

Lynn gestured absently. "They're around somewhere. Taylor said they had some last-minute presents to wrap. I think they're in one of the bedrooms."

As if on cue, Taylor and Wyatt wandered into the room. Taylor could usually be found elegantly groomed, every hair in place and her makeup beautifully applied. Now, though, her hair looked a little messy, her lipstick a little smudged and her eyes had the glow of a woman who had just been well and truly kissed.

Wrapping presents. Right, Kate thought, hiding her grin as Taylor caught sight of them, her brother and her best friend. She let out a distinctly inelegant whoop.

She slipped from Wyatt's arms and rushed to them, her arms outstretched. When she neared, she came to a dead stop, her eyes wide. Only then did Kate realize Hunter's fingers were entwined with hers, something that had become almost second nature to them in the last six days.

Taylor's gaze shifted rapidly from their joined hands to their faces in turn and then her shocked expression gave way to joy.

She hugged them both hard. "It's about time my brother got some sense," she whispered in Kate's ear when she embraced her.

"Everyone is here at last so we can start dinner," Lynn said. "Sit down, sit down."

"What about presents?" Gaby whined.

Allie shushed her. "Later. I've told you that a hundred times."

"At least," Gage murmured with a fond smile to his stepdaughters.

Everyone took their seats and Kate was grateful to see Lynn must have quickly set an extra place for Hunter—either that or she had suspected all along that Kate would bring him.

When everyone was gathered around the big pine table, Sam cleared his throat. "This is the most wonderful of Christmases. To have everyone together again seems like a miracle."

Everyone's gaze subtly shifted to Kate. A few days earlier she would have squirmed under their attention but now she only smiled.

"Before we say grace," Sam went on, "Lynn and I have an announcement."

He looked as nervous as a boy on his first date, she thought, as her father lifted her mother's hand above the table. "Lynn and I are, um, getting married again. Valentine's Day."

Both he and Lynn looked anxiously at their assembled family as if they thought they had dropped a bombshell on everyone. No one looked particularly surprised, though Kate might have been if she hadn't observed that furtive kiss in the kitchen.

With a sound of disgust, Wyatt reached into his pocket and pulled out a bill, then slapped it onto the table in front of Gage. "There you go. Twenty bucks."

"You bet on whether your parents would get back together?" Taylor asked, her voice outraged.

"No. We both figured out that was a given a long time ago. Gage said Valentine's Day. I thought Mom would hold out for a spring wedding."

Her big, tough FBI agent of a brother pocketed the money, a grin on his handsome features. "What can I say? I'm a romantic."

Wyatt snickered at that but subsided at a stern look from Taylor.

Kate remembered Hunter's proposal the night before when they had been throwing snowballs at each other outside their Wyoming hotel and her joyful acceptance. She thought of sharing the news with her family but decided she wanted to treasure it to herself for a while longer.

She was glad she said nothing when Allie spoke up quietly.

"We have news too." She reached for Gage's hand. "We're having a baby, due in June."

There were general exclamations of delight at the table.

"We might have a brother," Anna said.

"See, Mama," Gaby added, "I can *too* keep my mouth shut sometimes. I didn't tell anyone, not even Grandma Lynn."

Everyone laughed, but Taylor and Kate both honed in on Allie at the same time.

"Who's your OB?" Taylor asked.

"How is your pregnancy affecting your blood sugar?" Kate asked, concerned over Allie's diabetes.

"Does your doctor anticipate putting you on bed rest for the last trimester?" Taylor asked.

Allie looked a little overwhelmed by all the questions.

"This is what happens when you have two doctors in the family," Wyatt said with a laugh.

"And a nurse," Gage reminded them. "Allie knows how to take care of herself."

"The food's getting cold," Sam spoke up in his quiet way. "You can jabber all you want about babies and weddings while we're stuffing our faces but let's say grace so this feast your mother spent all day working on doesn't go to waste."

Kate smiled a little at Hunter's disconcerted expression when everyone reached around the table to hold hands with those on either side of them, but he reached for Taylor's fingers with his left hand and Kate's on his right.

She was seated next to Lynn and her mother's hand was smooth and soft, though she laced her fingers through Kate's tightly as Sam began to pray.

Her father's prayer was beautiful and heartfelt. He gave thanks for all the blessings the family had seen through the year, for new loves and second chances, and especially for the miracle of their little girl's return to them, after so many years of searching for her.

His voice broke a little at that point and he paused. Kate peeked under her eyelashes to find that tears seeped from both her parents' closed eyes—and even Gage and Wyatt looked suspiciously teary.

She was weeping a little, too, she realized, and her tears dripped even more freely when in his deep, quiet voice Sam gave thanks for those who had cared for her while she was away from them, who had showed her love when her family couldn't.

She thought of Maryanne and Tom, and at that moment she finally realized how truly blessed she was.

How many people had been gifted with two sets of loving parents? When she and Hunter married in a few months, she would have two kind, loving men to walk her down the aisle, two mothers to fuss over her gown and her veil. Even though Hunter's parents were dead, their children would still have two sets of grandparents to love them and spoil them.

She had two sets of parents, two brothers who loved her, two new sisters-in-law she loved dearly, a pair of beautiful new nieces.

And Hunter by her side, with his strength and his goodness and his love.

She was the luckiest woman in the world.

* * * * *

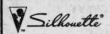

If you enjoyed what you just read,
then we've got an offer you can't resist!

Take 2 bestselling love stories FREE!

Plus get a FREE surprise gift!

COMING NEXT MONTH

INTIMATE MOMENTS

SIMCNM0505